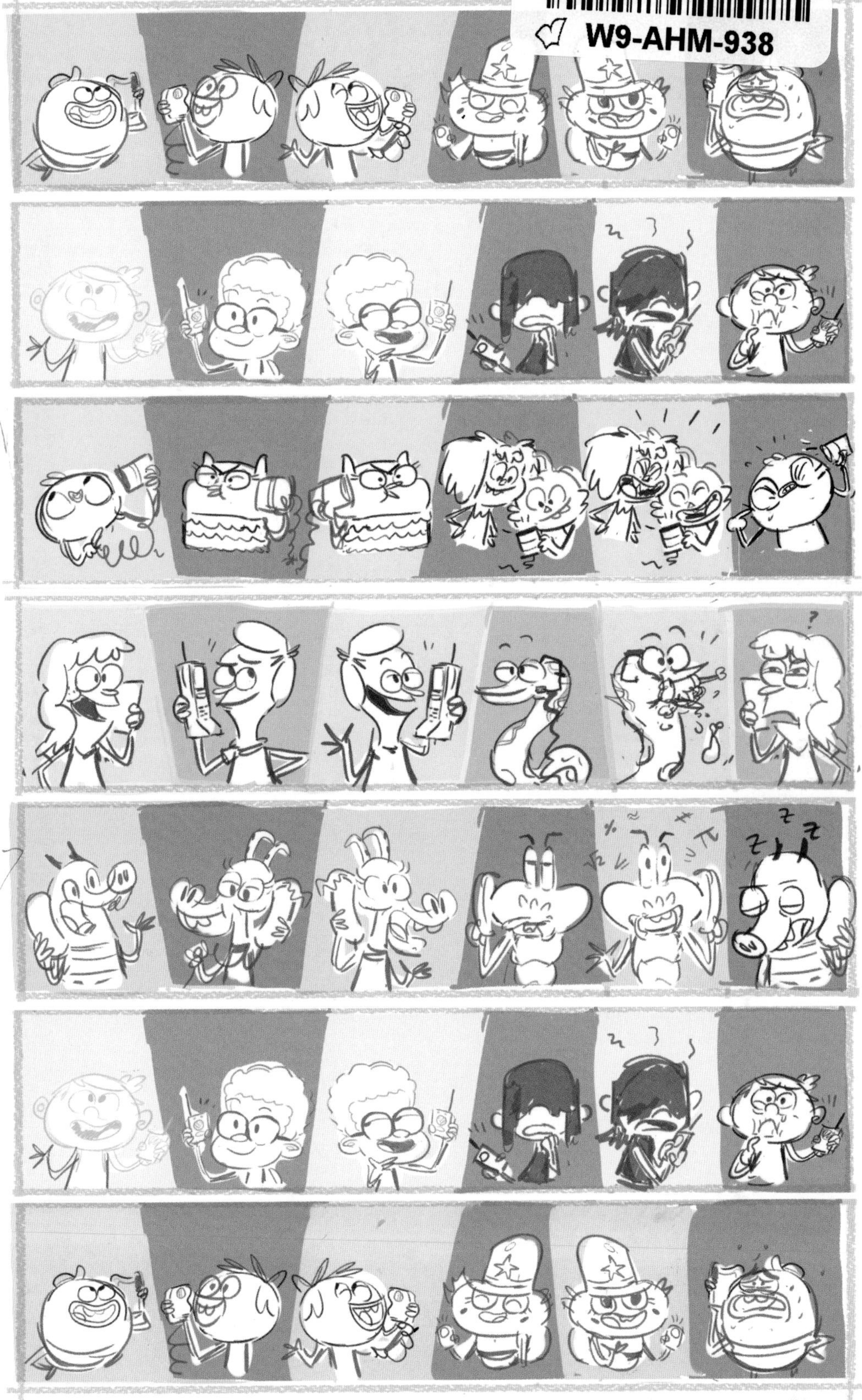

nickelodeon™

PANDEMONIUM!

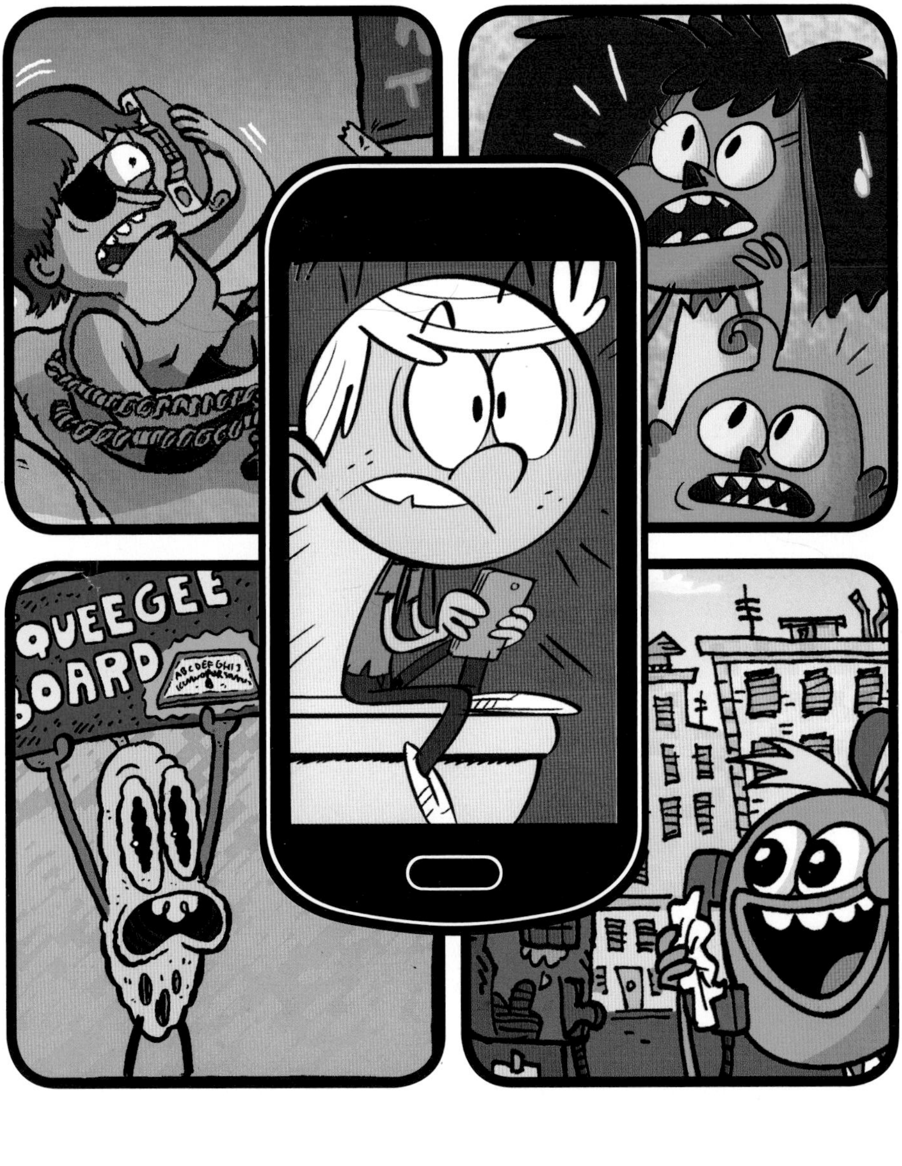
QUEEGEE
BOARD

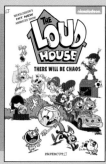

nickelodeon™
PANDEMONIUM!

Lucy's ABCs of the Loud House
5

Community Service
10

Fateway
19

Lower Yeast Side
20

Foo Facts #81- Fire
29

Tumors and Rumors
30

Close Encounters of the Spooky Kind
39

Mollusca Ducks
53

Foo Facts #67 Pirate Booty
55

In Space
56

WATCH OUT FOR PAPERCUTZ™
70

There Will Be Chaos Preview
71

nickelodeon

PANDEMONIUM!

#3 "RECEIVING YOU LOUD AND CLEAR"

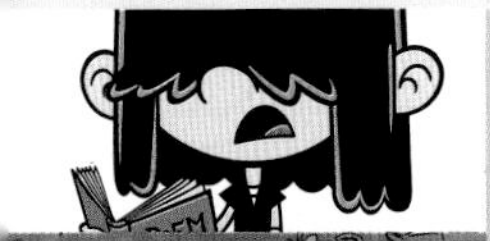

"LUCY'S ABCs OF THE LOUD HOUSE"
Karla Sakas Shropshire – Writer
Kiernan Sjursen-Lien – Artist, Letterer
Amanda Rynda – Colorist

"TUMORS AND RUMORS"
Eric Esquivel – Writer
James Kaminski – Artist
Laurie E. Smith – Colorist
Bryan Senka – Letterer

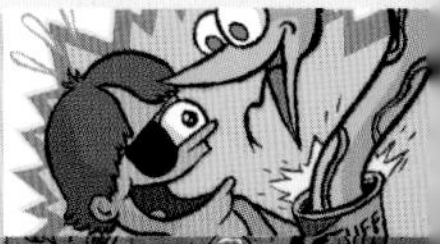

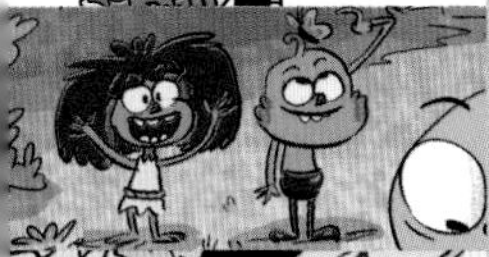

"COMMUNITY SERVICE"
David Scheidt – Writer
Andreas Schuster – Artist, Letterer
Laurie E. Smith – Colorist

"CLOSE ENCOUNTERS OF THE SPOOKY KIND"
Eric Esquivel – Writer
David DeGrand – Artist
Laurie E. Smith, Matt Herms – Colorists
Tom Orzechowski – Letterer

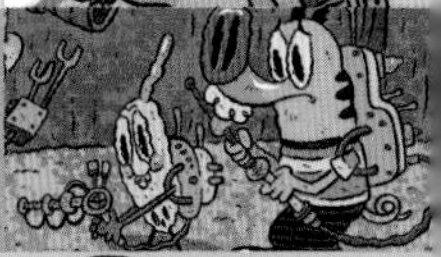

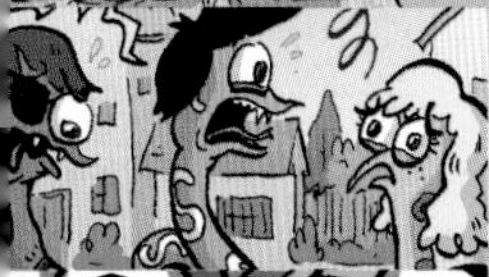

"FATEWAY"
Dale Malinowski – Writer
Sam Spina – Artist, Letterer
Laurie E. Smith – Colorist

"MOLLUSCA DUCKS"
Dale Malinowski – Writer
Gary Fields – Artist
Laurie E. Smith – Colorist
Bryan Senka – Letterer

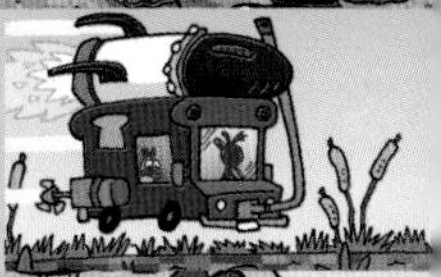

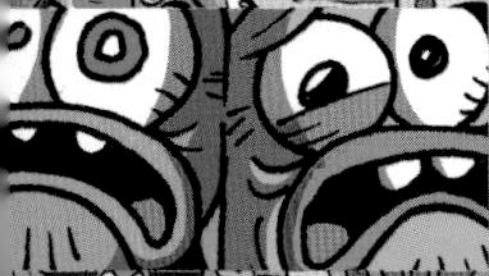

"LOWER YEAST SIDE"
Eric Esquivel – Writer
Gary Fields – Artist
Laurie E. Smith – Colorist
Bryan Senka – Letterer

"FOO FACTS #67 – PIRATE BOOTY"
Carson Montgomery – Writer
Andreas Schuster – Artist, Colorist, Letterer

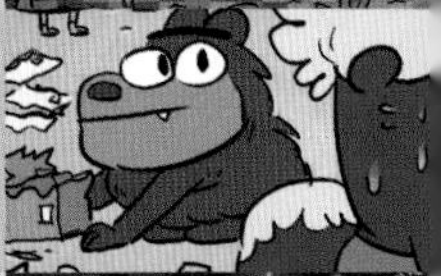

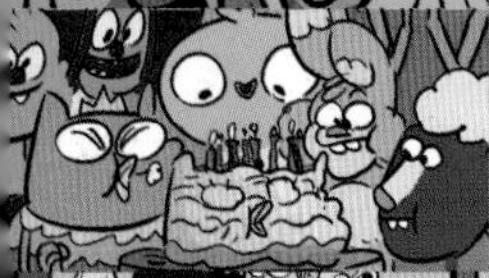

"FOO FACTS #81– FIRE"
Carson Montgomery – Writer
Andreas Schuster – Artist, Colorist, Letterer

"PIG GOAT BANANA CRICKET IN SPACE"
Eric Esquivel – Writer
Andreas Schuster – Artist, Letterer
Matt Herms, Laurie E. Smith – Colorists

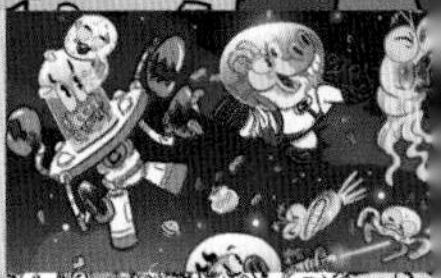

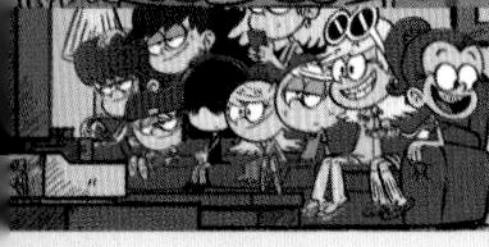

"SHOCKER"
Miguel Puga – Writer, Artist, Letterer
Amanda Rynda – Colorist

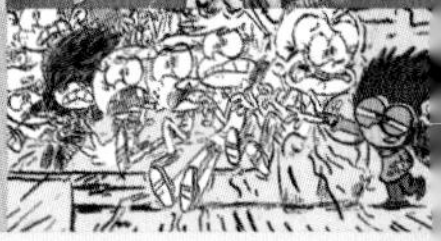

Breadwinners created by Gary "Doodles" DiRaffeale and Steve Borst
Harvey Beaks created by C.H. Greenblatt
Pig Goat Banana Cricket created by Johnny Ryan and Dave Cooper
Sanjay and Craig created by Jim Dirschberger, Jay Howell, and Andreas Trolf
The Loud House created by Chris Savino
Chris Savino and Andreas Schuster – Cover Artists
James Salerno – Sr. Art Director/Nickelodeon
Dawn Guzzo – Design/Production Coordination
Jeff Whitman – Editor
Joan Hilty – Comics Editor/Nickelodeon
Jim Salicrup
Editor-in-Chief

ISBN: 978-1-62991-755-9 paperback edition
ISBN: 978-1-62991-756-6 hardcover edition

Papercutz books may be purchased for business or promotional use. For information on bulk purchases please contact Macmillan Corporate and Premium Sales Department at (800) 221-7945 x5442.

Printed in China
August 2017

Distributed by Macmillan
First Printing

"LUCY'S ABCs OF THE LOUD HOUSE"

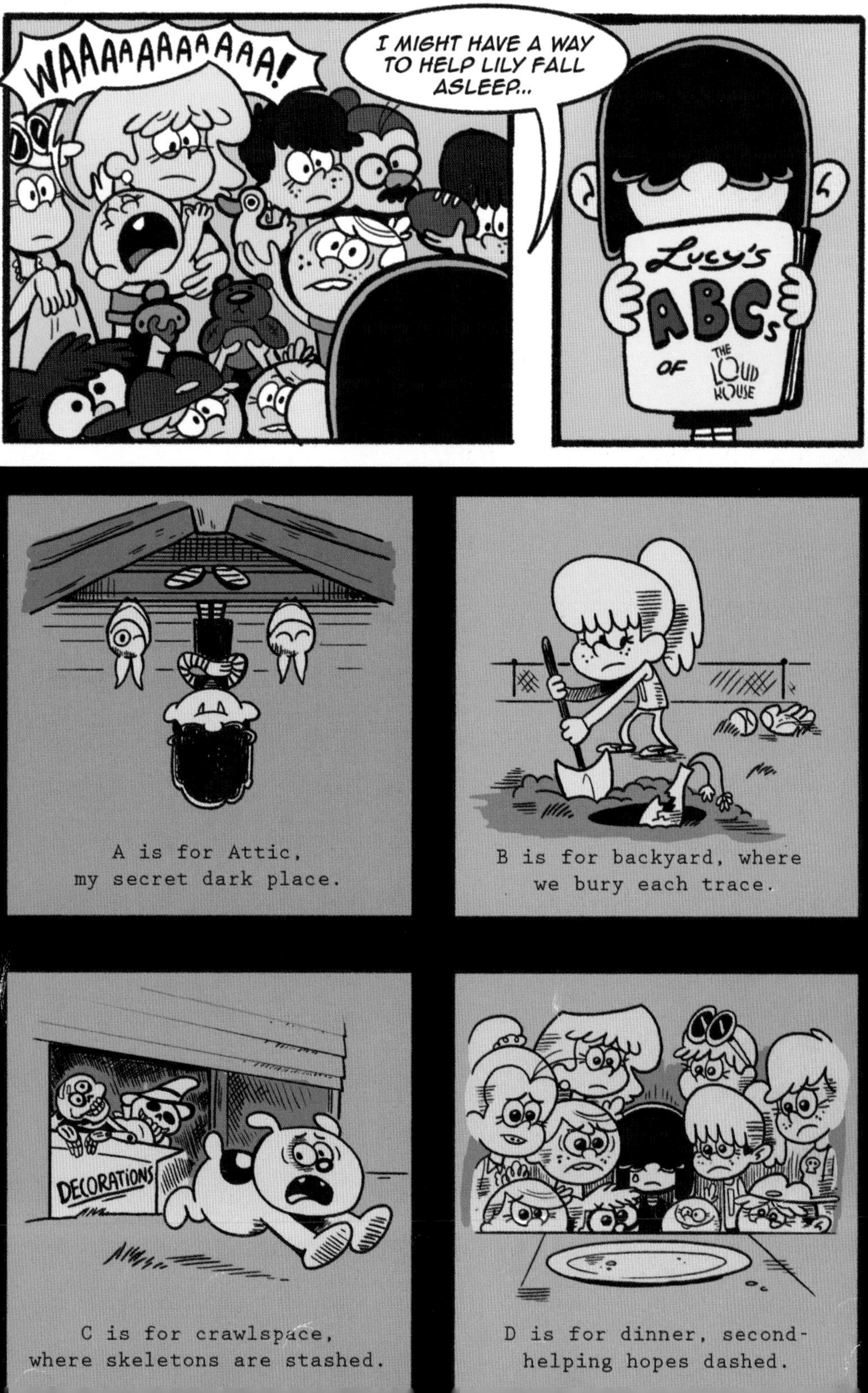

WAAAAAAAAAA!
I MIGHT HAVE A WAY TO HELP LILY FALL ASLEEP...
Lucy's ABCs OF THE LOUD HOUSE
A is for Attic,
my secret dark place.
B is for backyard, where
we bury each trace.
DECORATIONS
C is for crawlspace,
where skeletons are stashed.
D is for dinner, second-
helping hopes dashed.

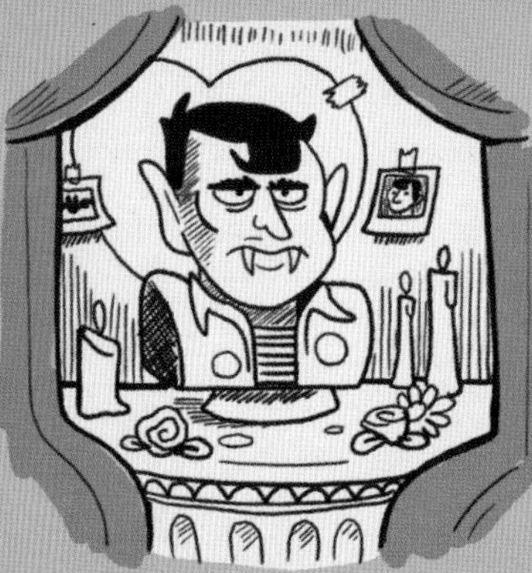

E is for Edwin shrine,
safe in my room.

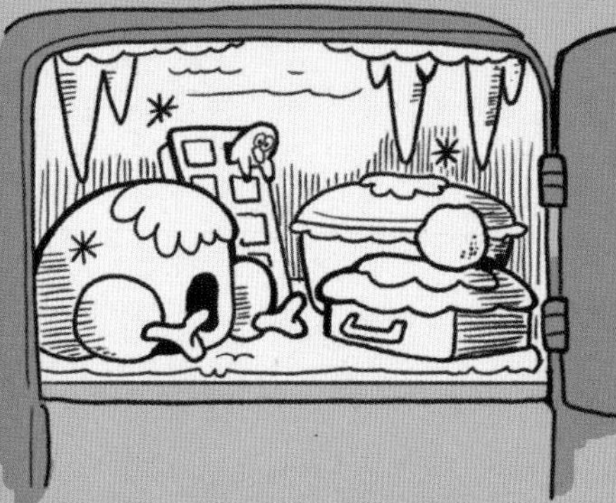

F is for freezer, where
leftovers meet their doom.

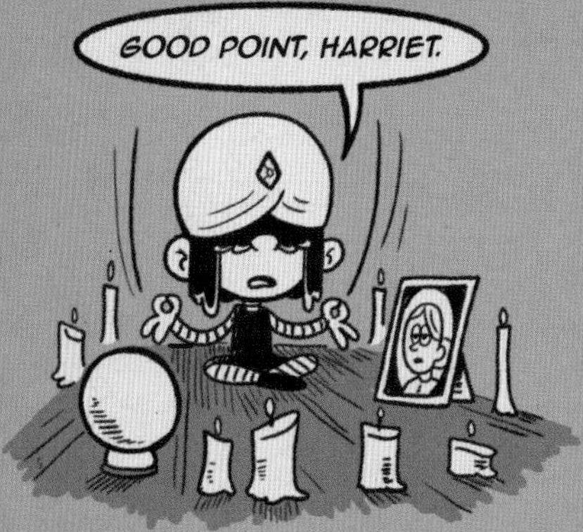
GOOD POINT, HARRIET.

G is for Great Grandma,
of whom I'm so fond.

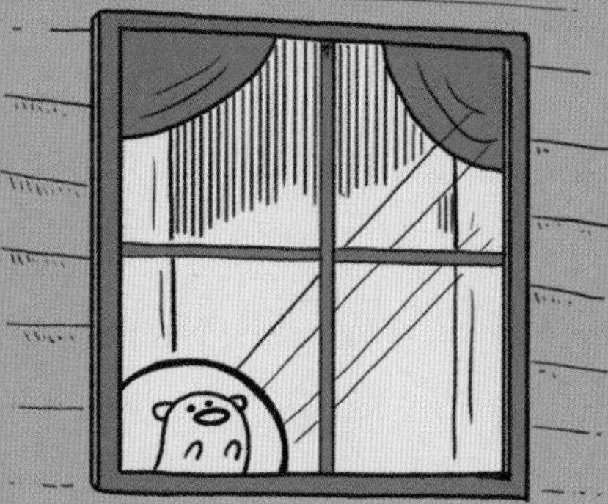

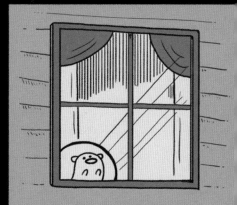

H is for hamster ball,
Geo can't get beyond.

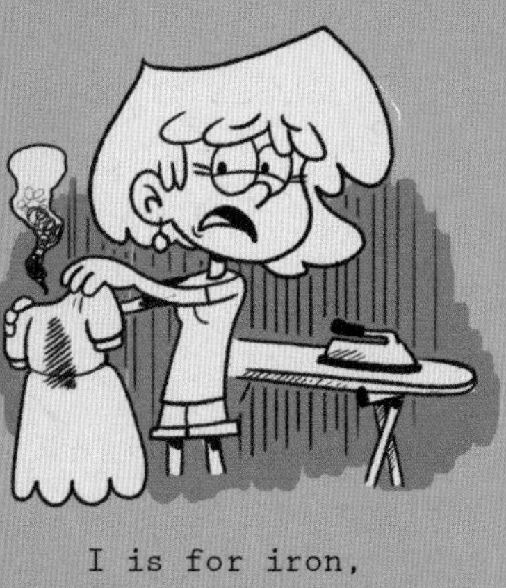

I is for iron,
feared by our clothes.

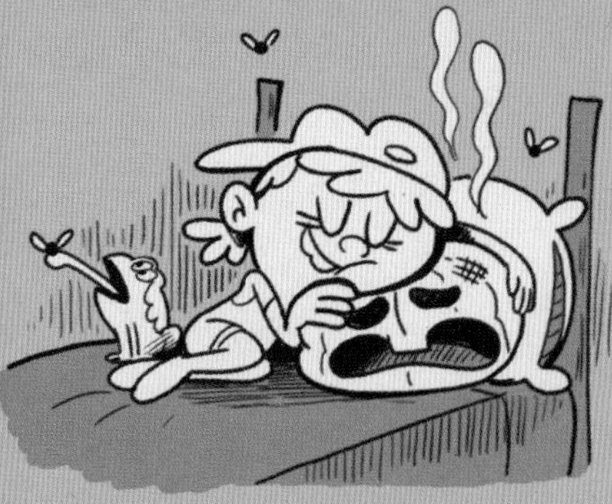

J is for Jack-O-Lantern
that got really gross.

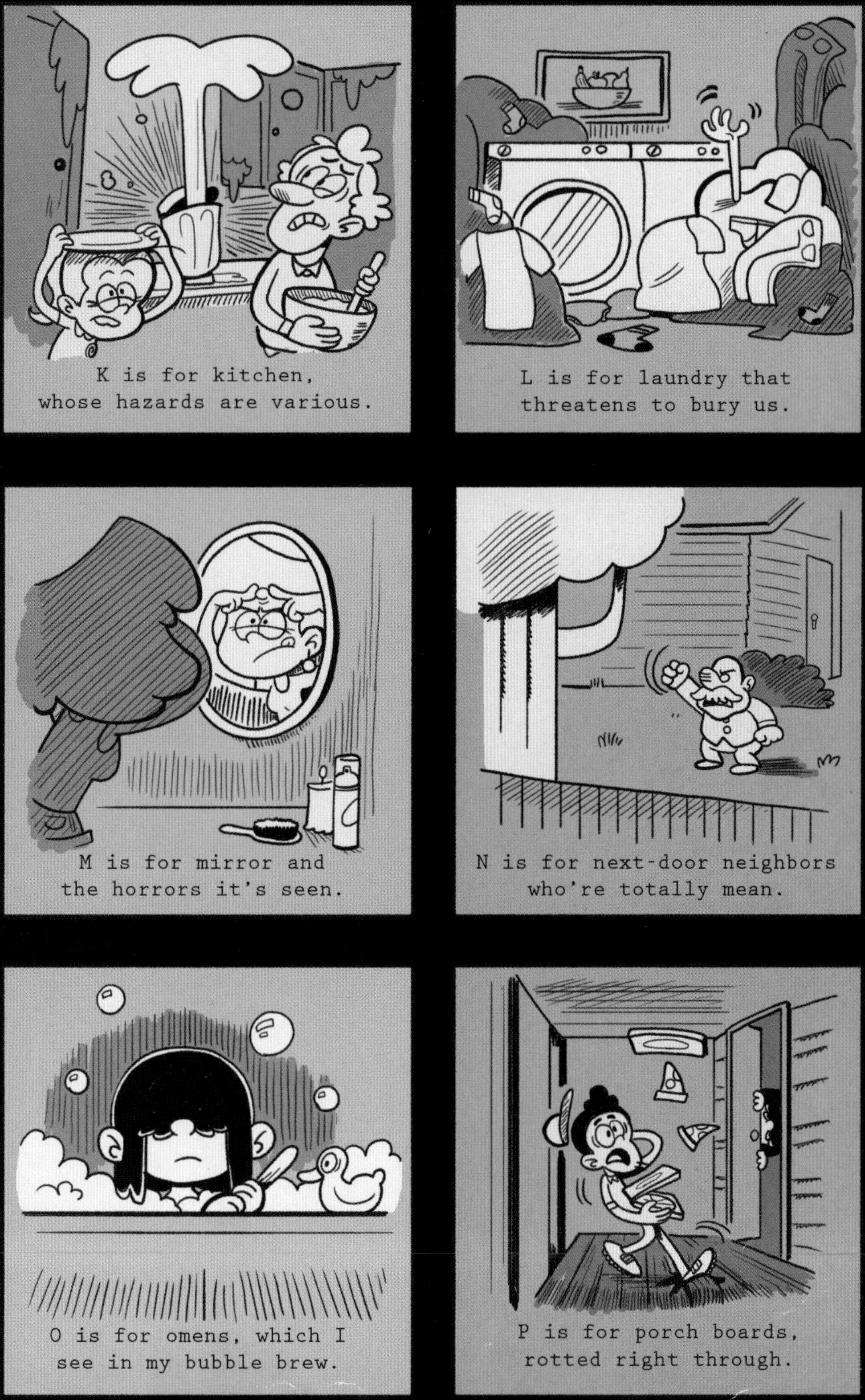
K is for kitchen,
whose hazards are various.
L is for laundry that
threatens to bury us.
M is for mirror and
the horrors it's seen.
N is for next-door neighbors
who're totally mean.
O is for omens, which I
see in my bubble brew.
P is for porch boards,
rotted right through.

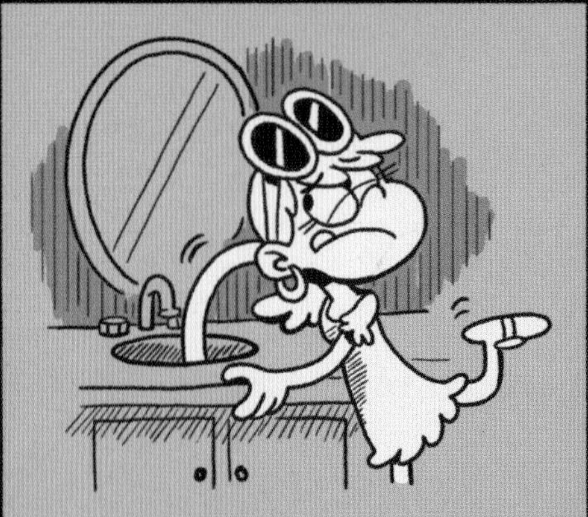

Q is for quarters
lost down the drain.

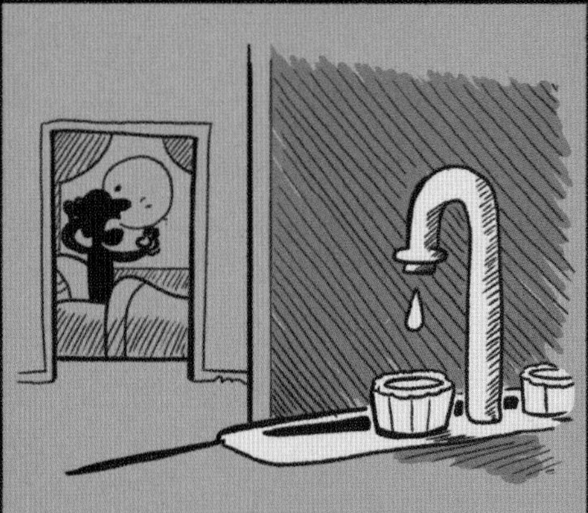

R is for runny faucet-
it drives Dad insane!

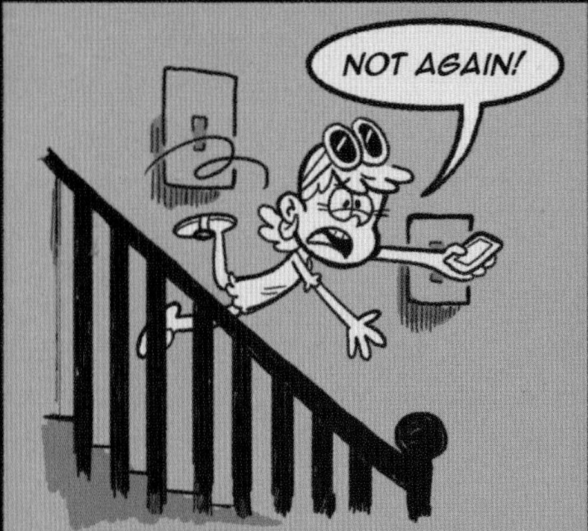
NOT AGAIN!

S is for staircase,
where Leni pratfalls.

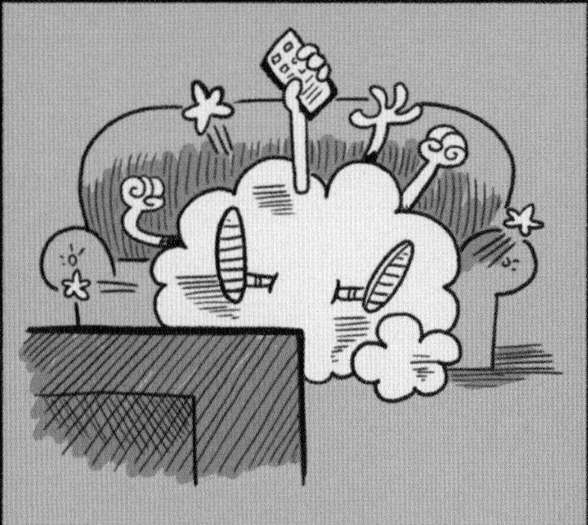

T is for TV remote,
which causes brawls.

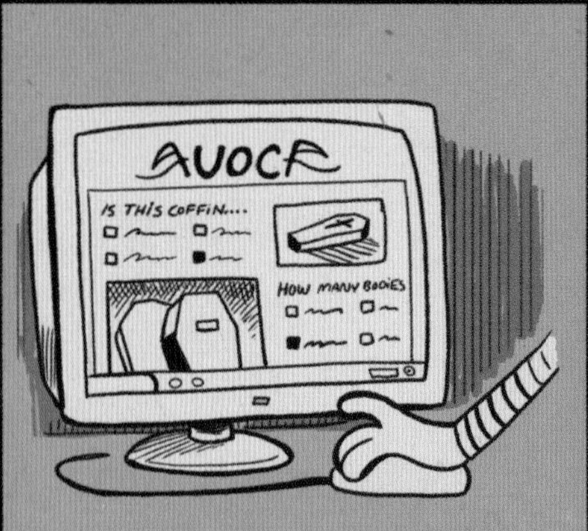
AUOCF
IS THIS COFFIN....
HOW MANY BODIES

U is for undertaker's
online course...

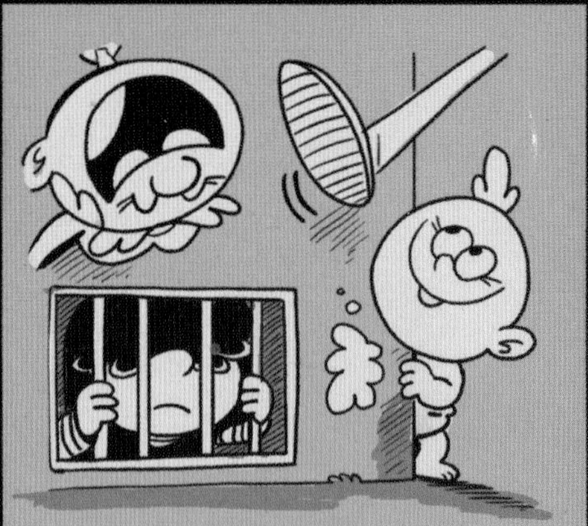

V is for vents, when
chaos is in full force.

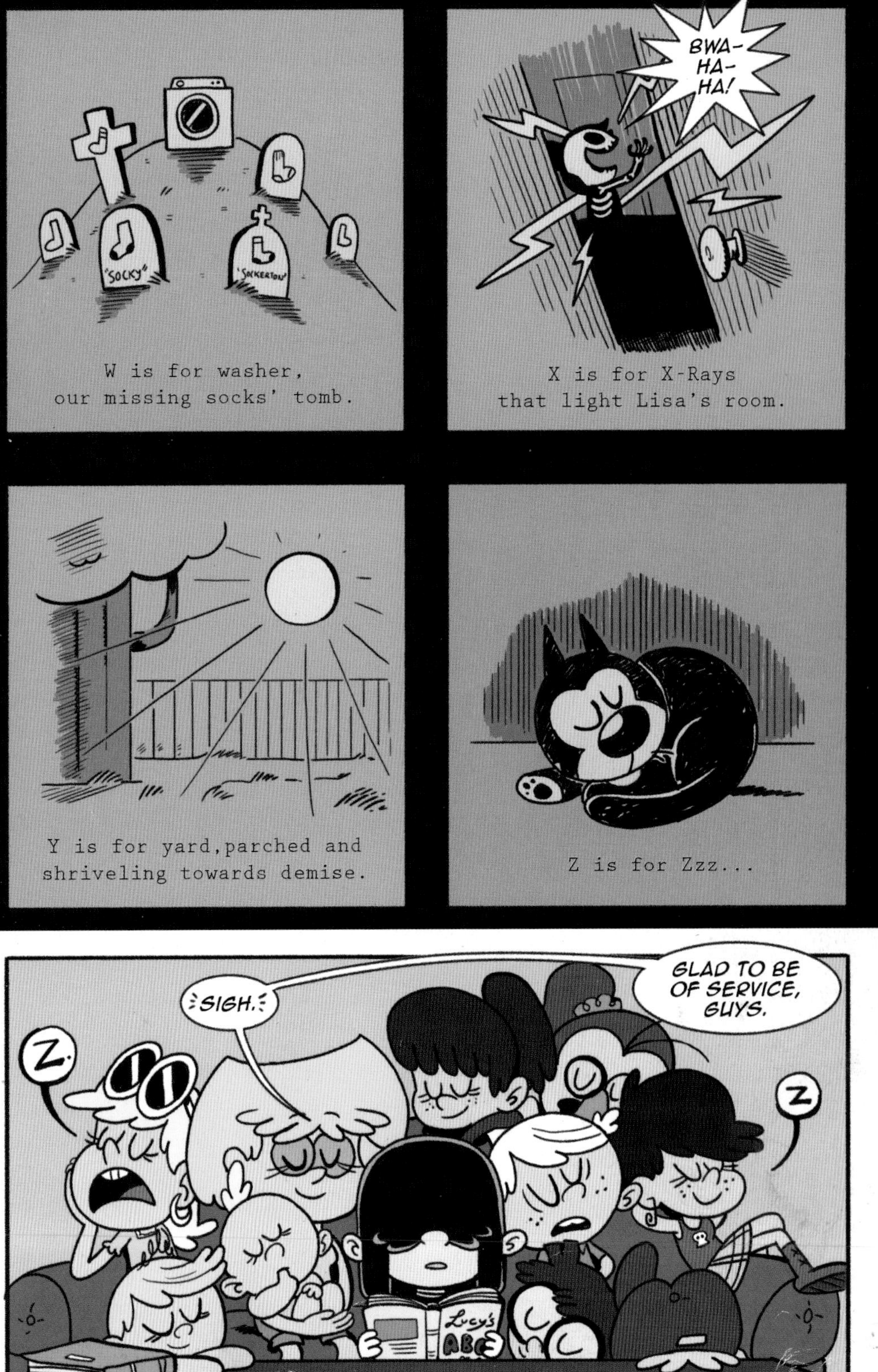
"SOCKY"
"SOCKERTON"
W is for washer,
our missing socks' tomb.
BWA-HA-HA!
X is for X-Rays
that light Lisa's room.
Y is for yard,parched and
shriveling towards demise.
Z is for Zzz...
Z
SIGH.
GLAD TO BE OF SERVICE, GUYS.
Z
Lucy's ABC

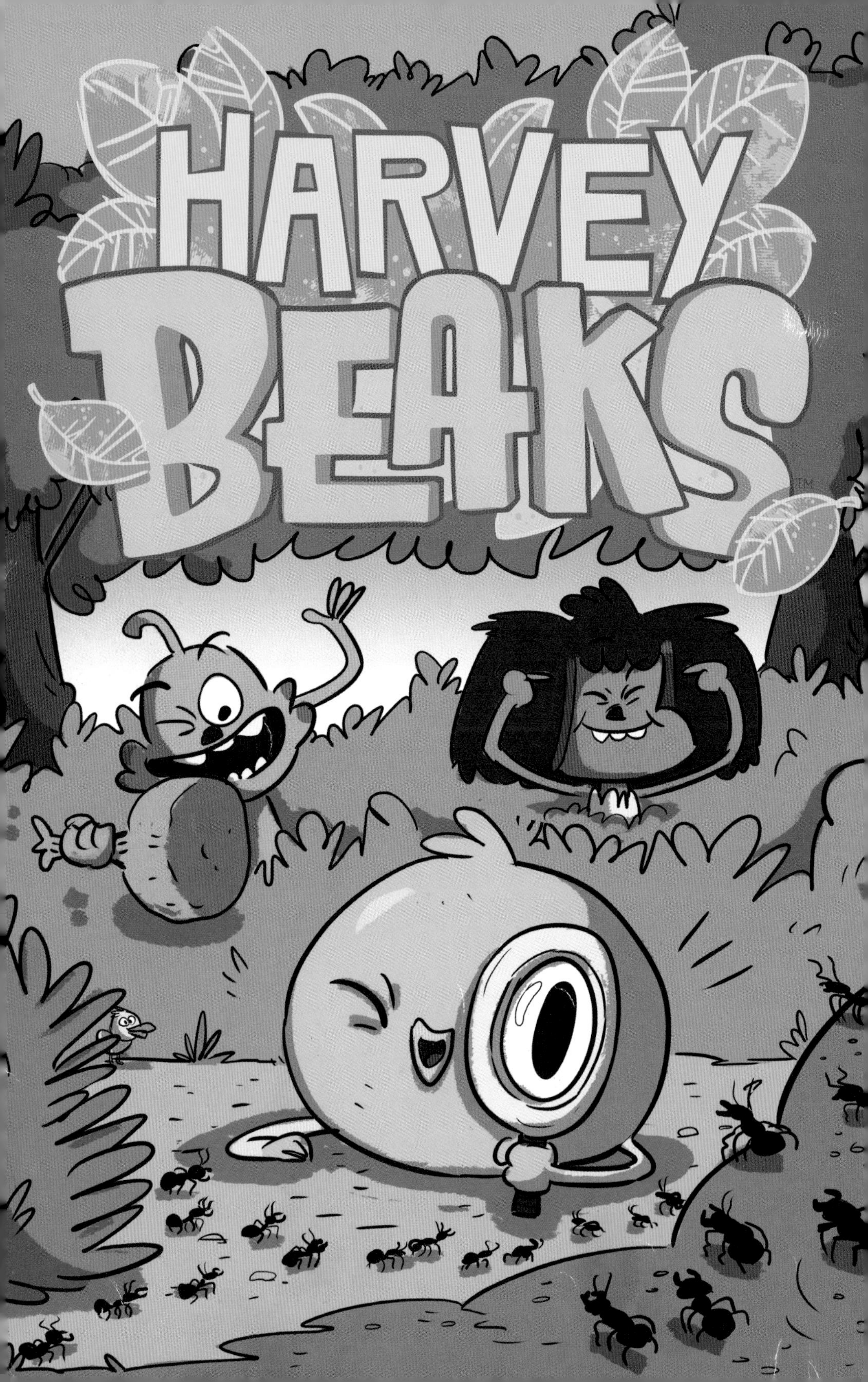
HARVEY BEAKS™

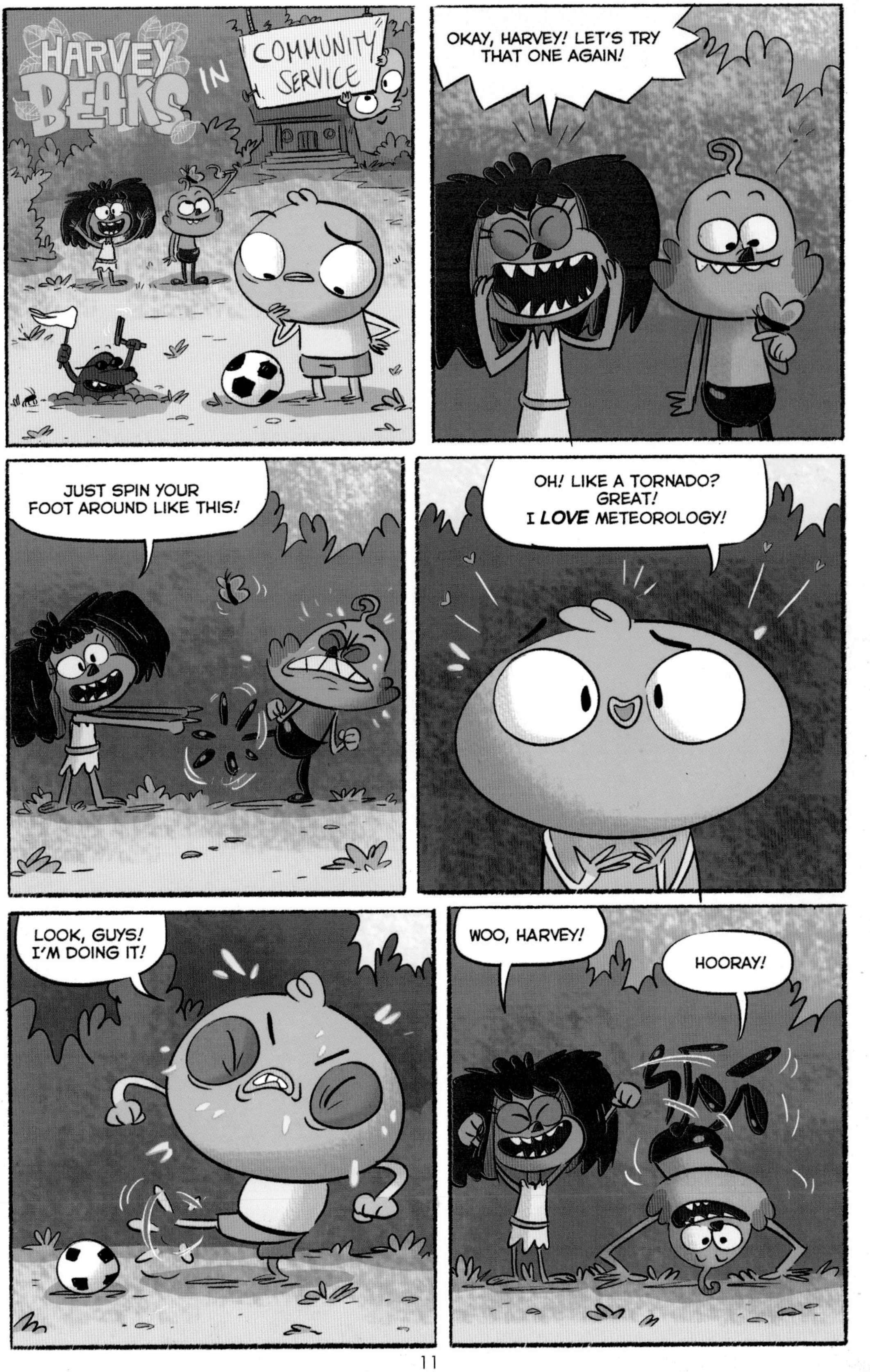
HARVEY BEAKS IN
COMMUNITY SERVICE
OKAY, HARVEY! LET'S TRY THAT ONE AGAIN!
JUST SPIN YOUR FOOT AROUND LIKE THIS!
OH! LIKE A TORNADO? GREAT! I LOVE METEOROLOGY!
LOOK, GUYS! I'M DOING IT!
WOO, HARVEY!
HOORAY!

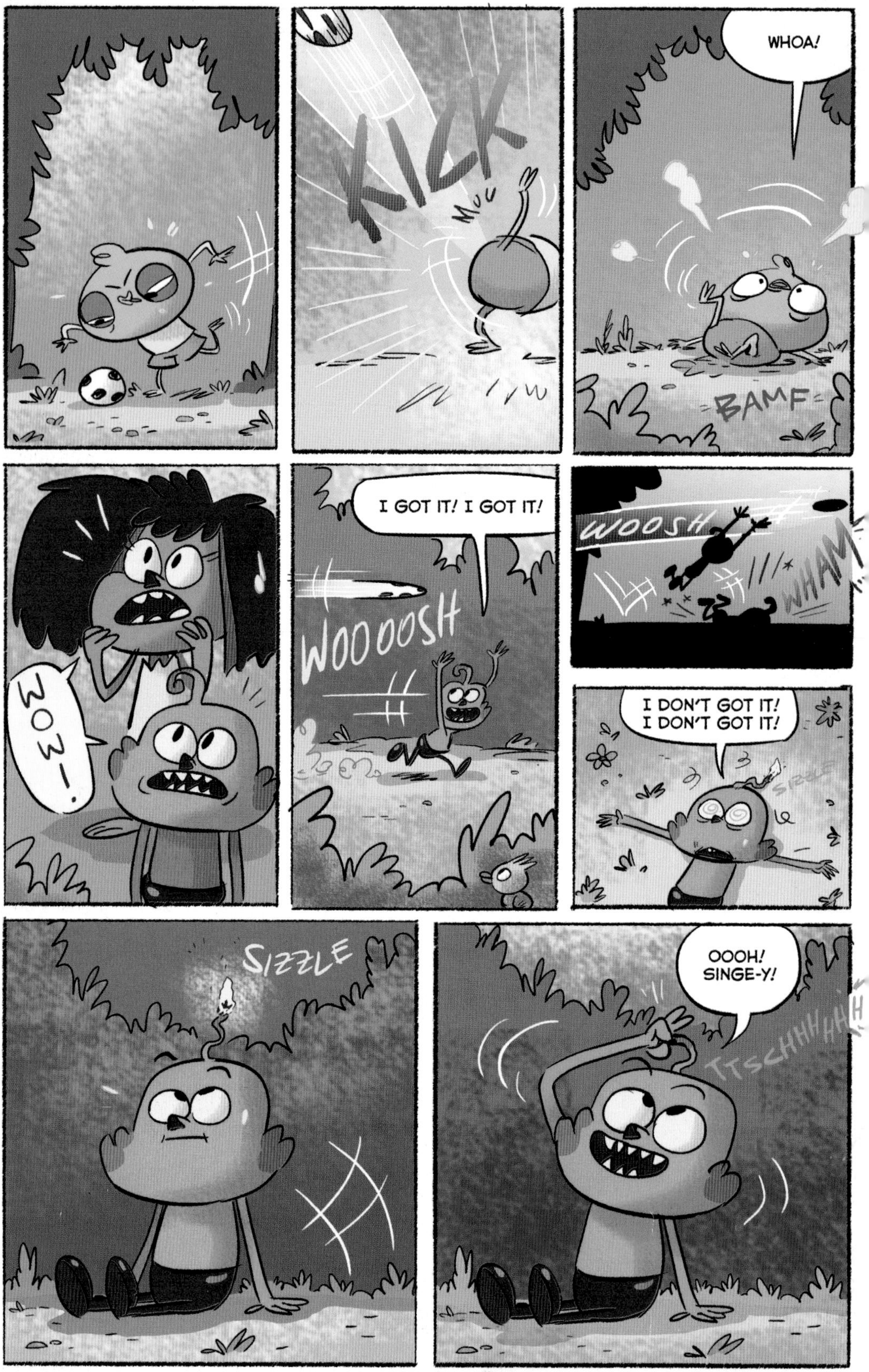
KICK
WHOA!
BAMF
WOW!
I GOT IT! I GOT IT!
WOOOOSH
WOOSH
WHAM
I DON'T GOT IT!
I DON'T GOT IT!
SIZZLE
SIZZLE
OOOH!
SINGE-Y!
TTSCHHHHHH

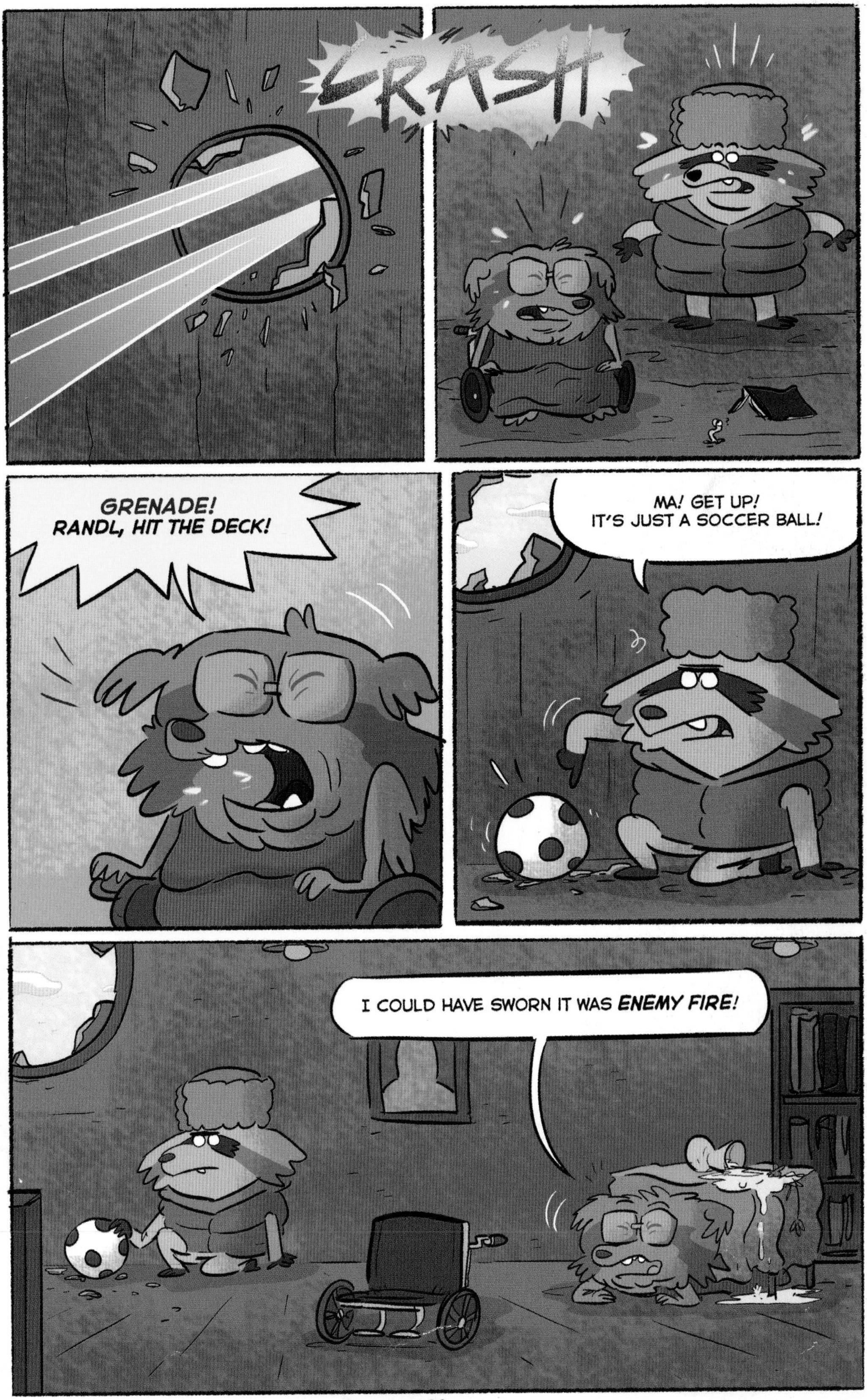
CRASH
GRENADE! RANDL, HIT THE DECK!
MA! GET UP! IT'S JUST A SOCCER BALL!
I COULD HAVE SWORN IT WAS ENEMY FIRE!

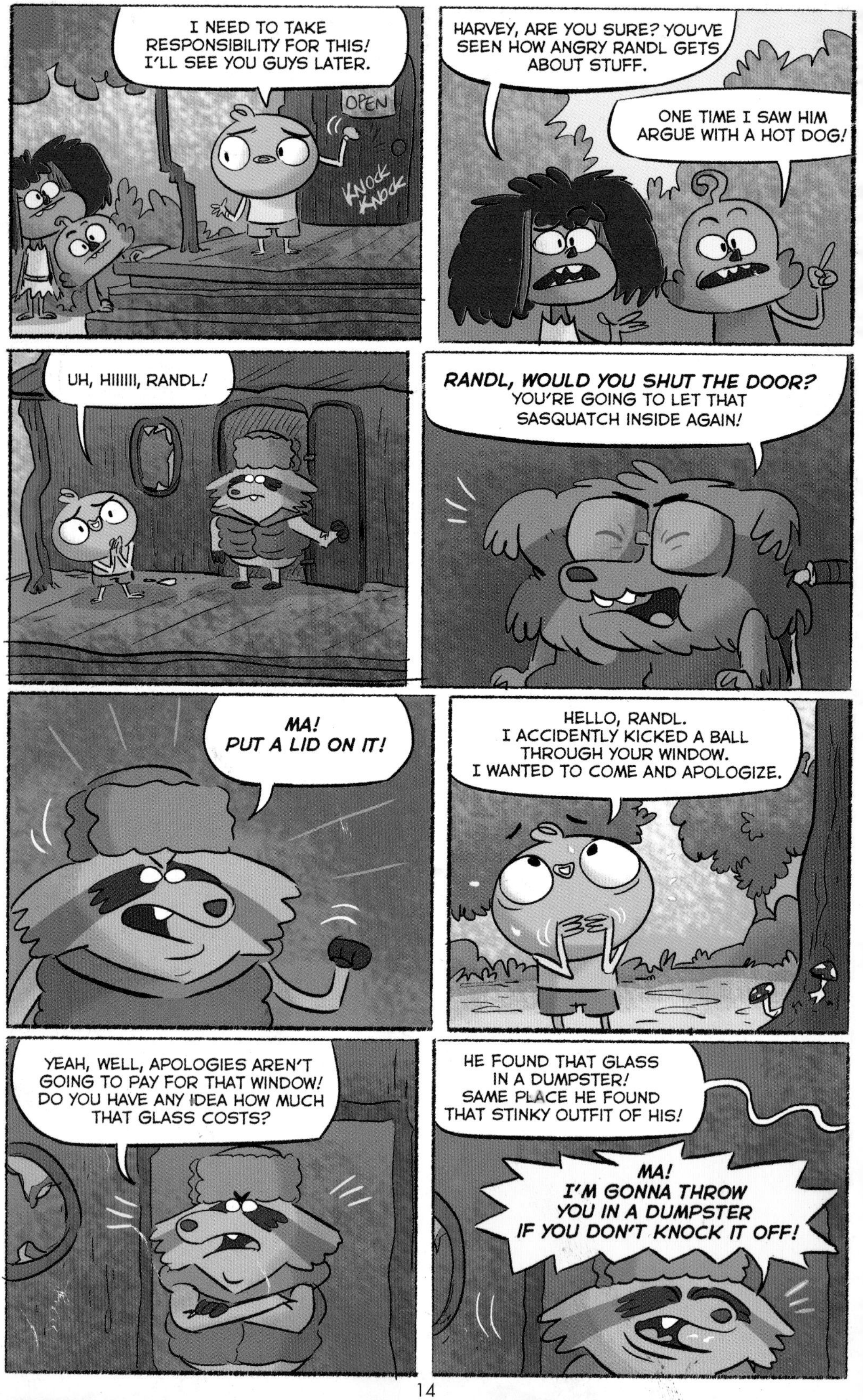
I NEED TO TAKE RESPONSIBILITY FOR THIS! I'LL SEE YOU GUYS LATER.
OPEN
KNOCK KNOCK
HARVEY, ARE YOU SURE? YOU'VE SEEN HOW ANGRY RANDL GETS ABOUT STUFF.
ONE TIME I SAW HIM ARGUE WITH A HOT DOG!
UH, HIIIIII, RANDL!
RANDL, WOULD YOU SHUT THE DOOR? YOU'RE GOING TO LET THAT SASQUATCH INSIDE AGAIN!
MA! PUT A LID ON IT!
HELLO, RANDL. I ACCIDENTLY KICKED A BALL THROUGH YOUR WINDOW. I WANTED TO COME AND APOLOGIZE.
YEAH, WELL, APOLOGIES AREN'T GOING TO PAY FOR THAT WINDOW! DO YOU HAVE ANY IDEA HOW MUCH THAT GLASS COSTS?
HE FOUND THAT GLASS IN A DUMPSTER! SAME PLACE HE FOUND THAT STINKY OUTFIT OF HIS!
MA! I'M GONNA THROW YOU IN A DUMPSTER IF YOU DON'T KNOCK IT OFF!

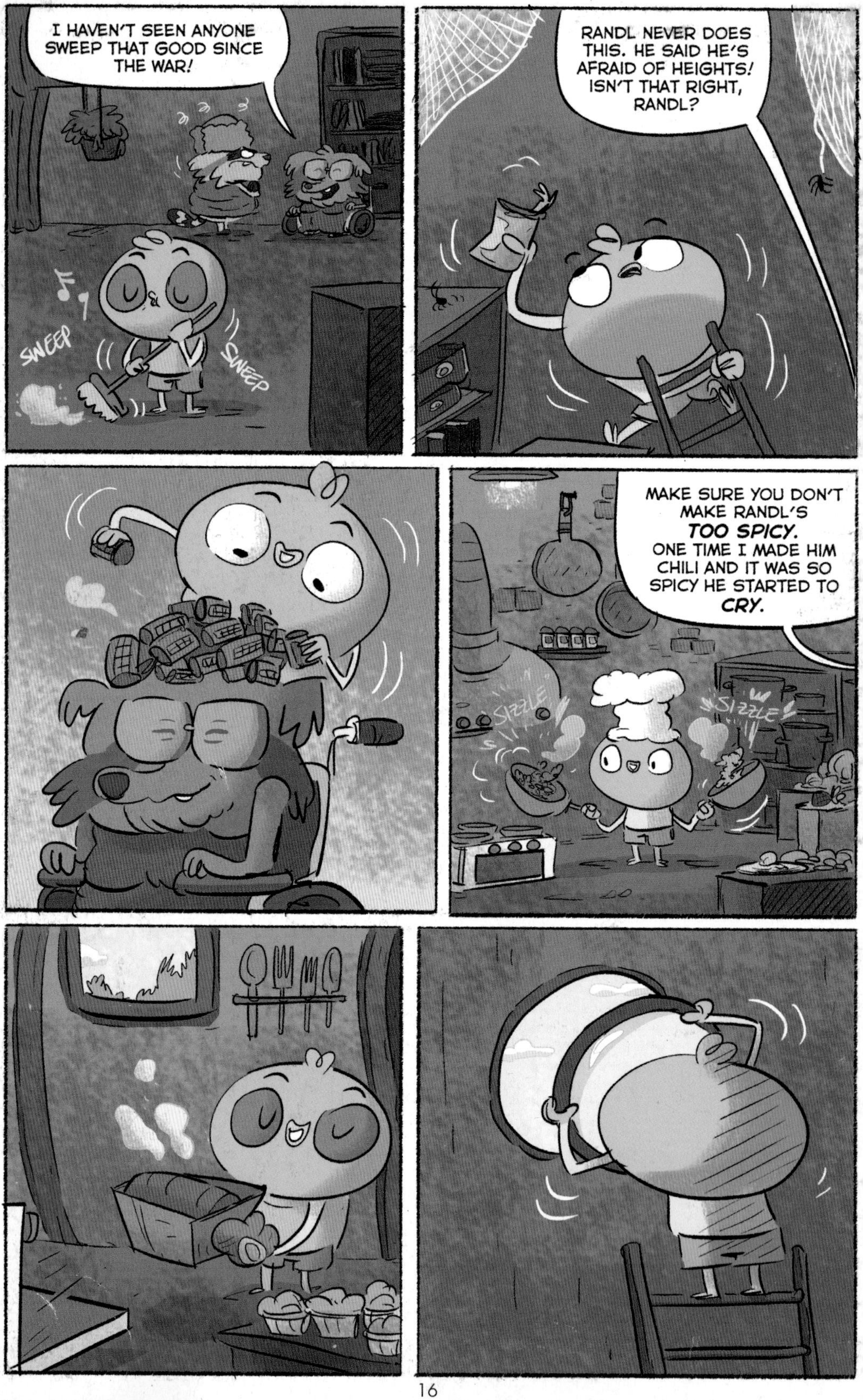
I HAVEN'T SEEN ANYONE SWEEP THAT GOOD SINCE THE WAR!
SWEEP
SWEEP
RANDL NEVER DOES THIS. HE SAID HE'S AFRAID OF HEIGHTS! ISN'T THAT RIGHT, RANDL?
MAKE SURE YOU DON'T MAKE RANDL'S **TOO SPICY.** ONE TIME I MADE HIM CHILI AND IT WAS SO SPICY HE STARTED TO **CRY.**
SIZZLE
SIZZLE

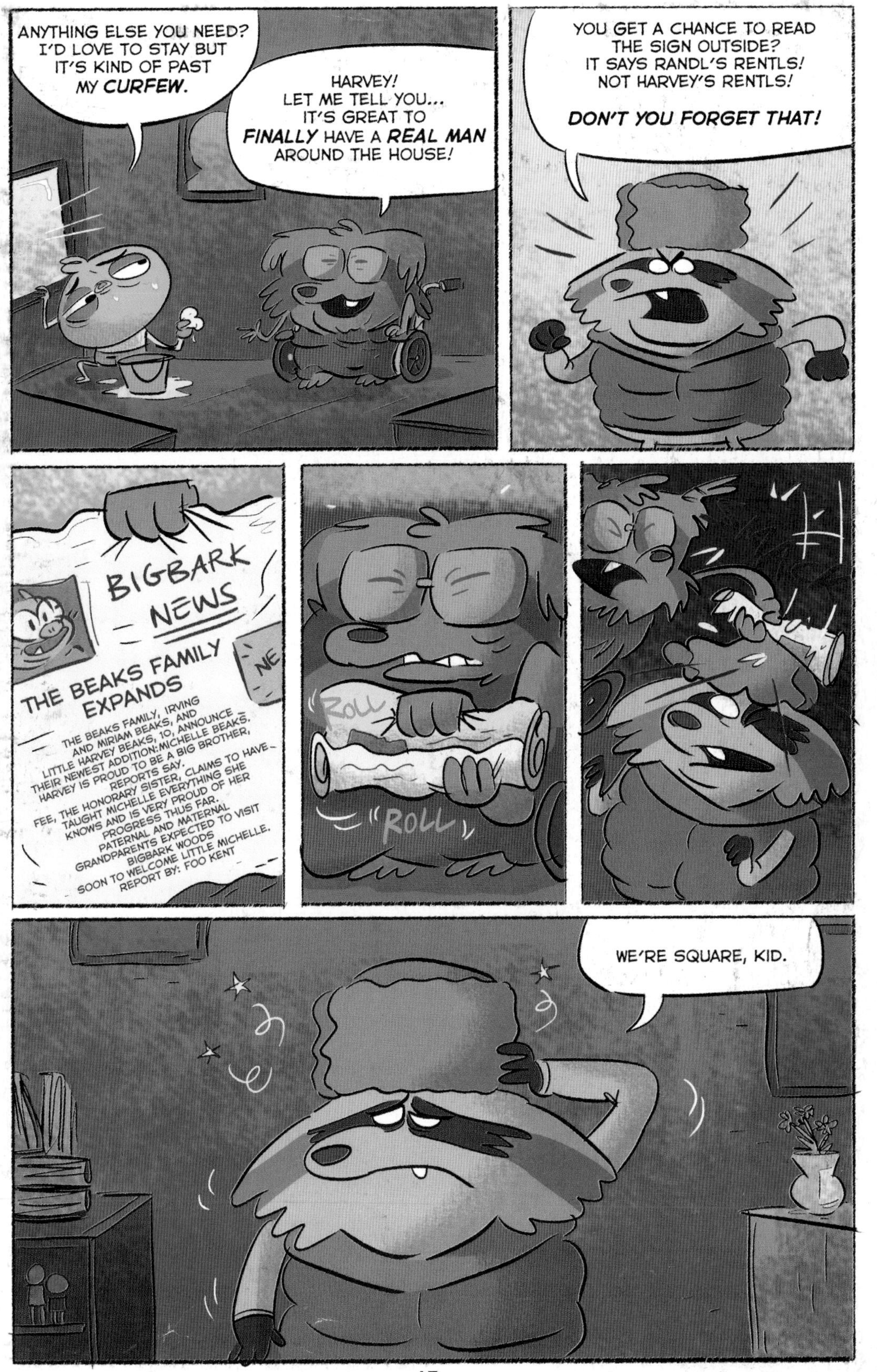
ANYTHING ELSE YOU NEED? I'D LOVE TO STAY BUT IT'S KIND OF PAST MY CURFEW.
HARVEY! LET ME TELL YOU... IT'S GREAT TO FINALLY HAVE A REAL MAN AROUND THE HOUSE!
YOU GET A CHANCE TO READ THE SIGN OUTSIDE? IT SAYS RANDL'S RENTLS! NOT HARVEY'S RENTLS!
DON'T YOU FORGET THAT!
BIGBARK NEWS
THE BEAKS FAMILY EXPANDS
THE BEAKS FAMILY, IRVING AND MIRIAM BEAKS, AND LITTLE HARVEY BEAKS, 10, ANNOUNCE THEIR NEWEST ADDITION: MICHELLE BEAKS. HARVEY IS PROUD TO BE A BIG BROTHER, REPORTS SAY.
FEE, THE HONORARY SISTER, CLAIMS TO HAVE TAUGHT MICHELLE EVERYTHING SHE KNOWS AND IS VERY PROUD OF HER PROGRESS THUS FAR.
PATERNAL AND MATERNAL GRANDPARENTS EXPECTED TO VISIT BIGBARK WOODS SOON TO WELCOME LITTLE MICHELLE.
REPORT BY: FOO KENT
ROLL
ROLL
WE'RE SQUARE, KID.

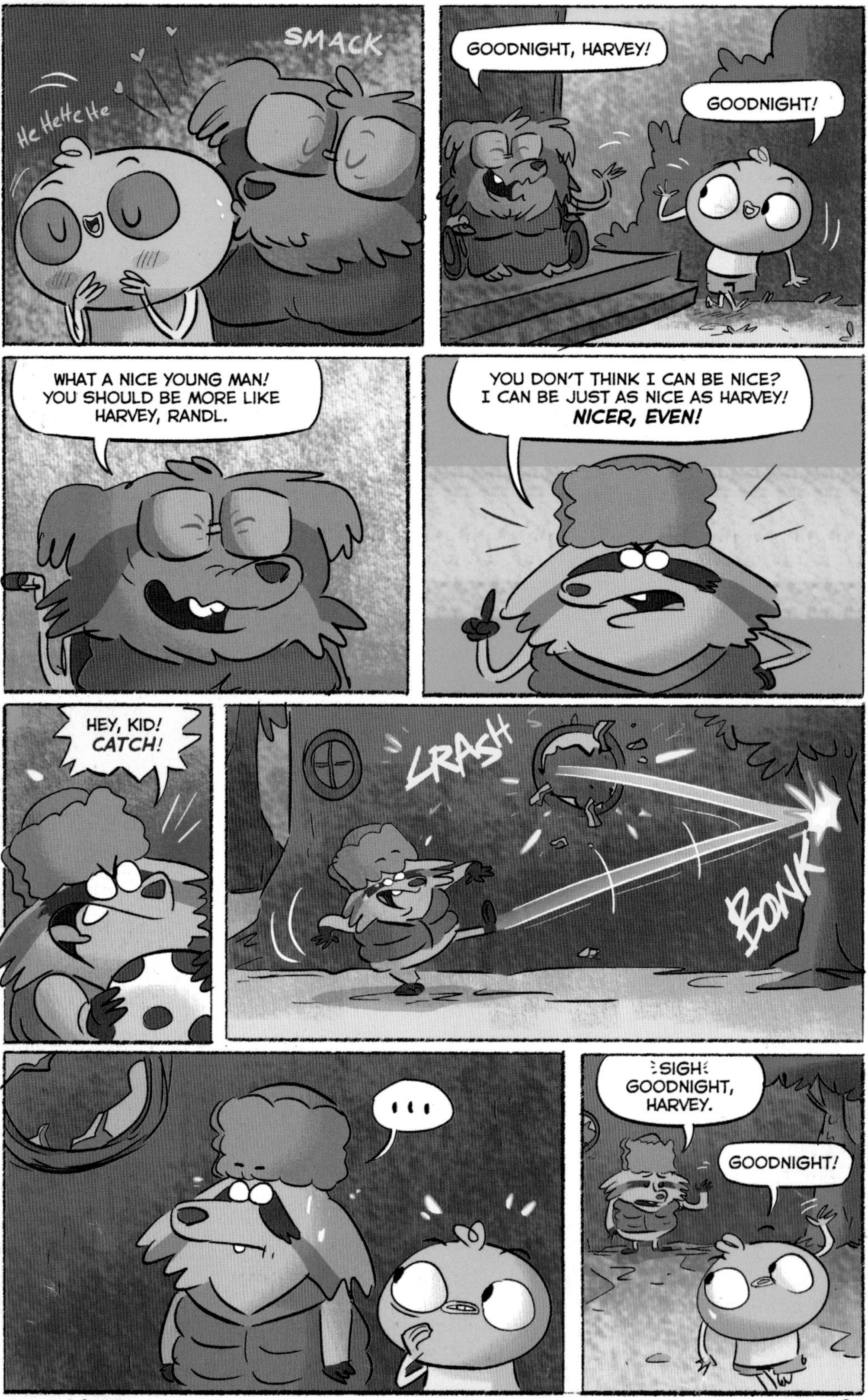

SMACK
He HeHe He
GOODNIGHT, HARVEY!
GOODNIGHT!
WHAT A NICE YOUNG MAN! YOU SHOULD BE MORE LIKE HARVEY, RANDL.
YOU DON'T THINK I CAN BE NICE? I CAN BE JUST AS NICE AS HARVEY! NICER, EVEN!
HEY, KID! CATCH!
CRASH
BONK
...
SIGH GOODNIGHT, HARVEY.
GOODNIGHT!

SCHEIDT & SCHUSTER

THE END

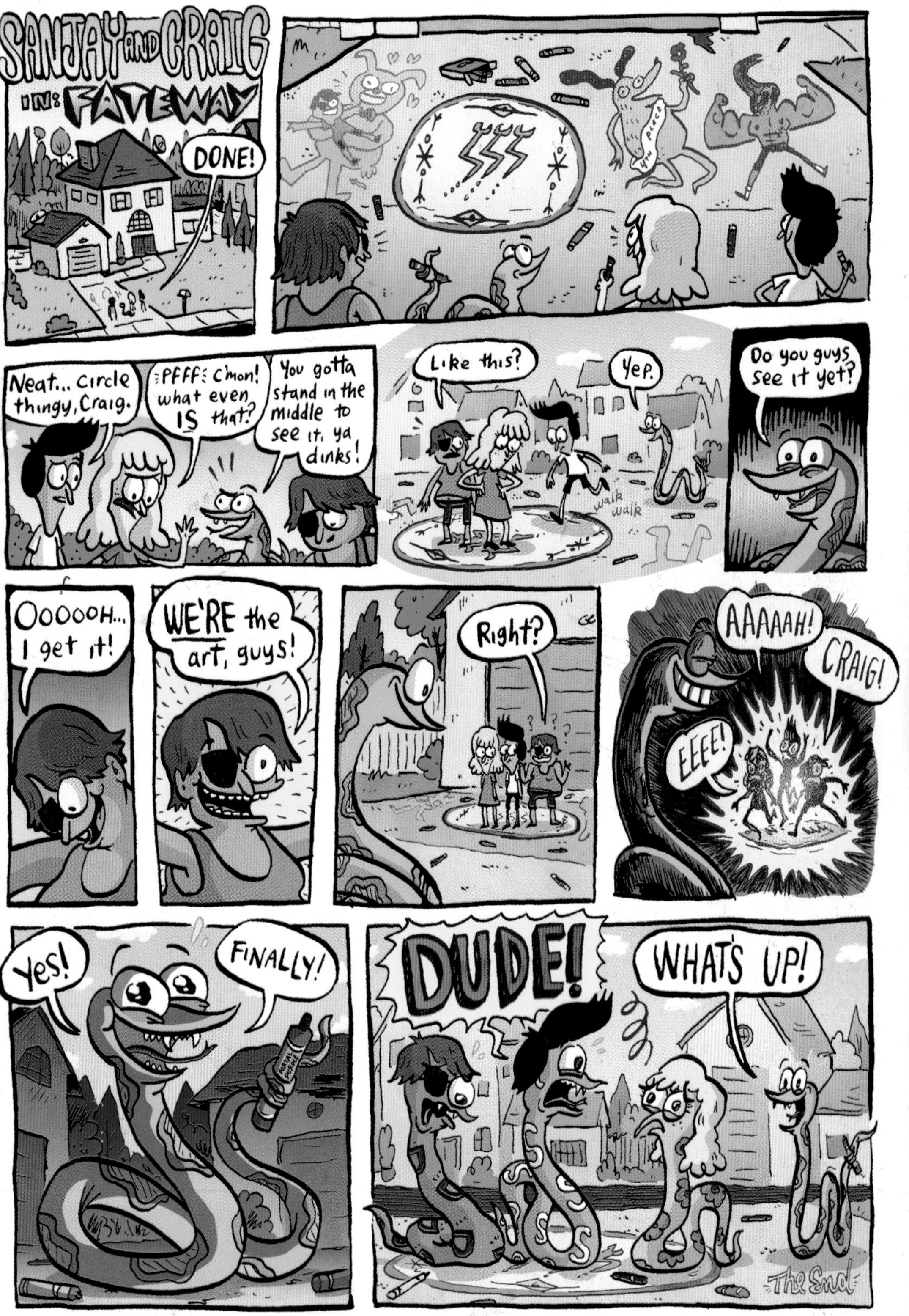
SANJAY AND CRAIG
IN: FATEWAY
DONE!
4th place
Neat... circle thingy, Craig.
PFFF! C'mon! what even IS that?
You gotta stand in the middle to see it, ya dinks!
Like this?
Yep.
walk walk
Do you guys see it yet?
OOOOOH... I get it!
WE'RE the art, guys!
Right?
AAAAAH!
CRAIG!
EEEE!
Yes!
FINALLY!
DUDE!
WHAT'S UP!
The Snd

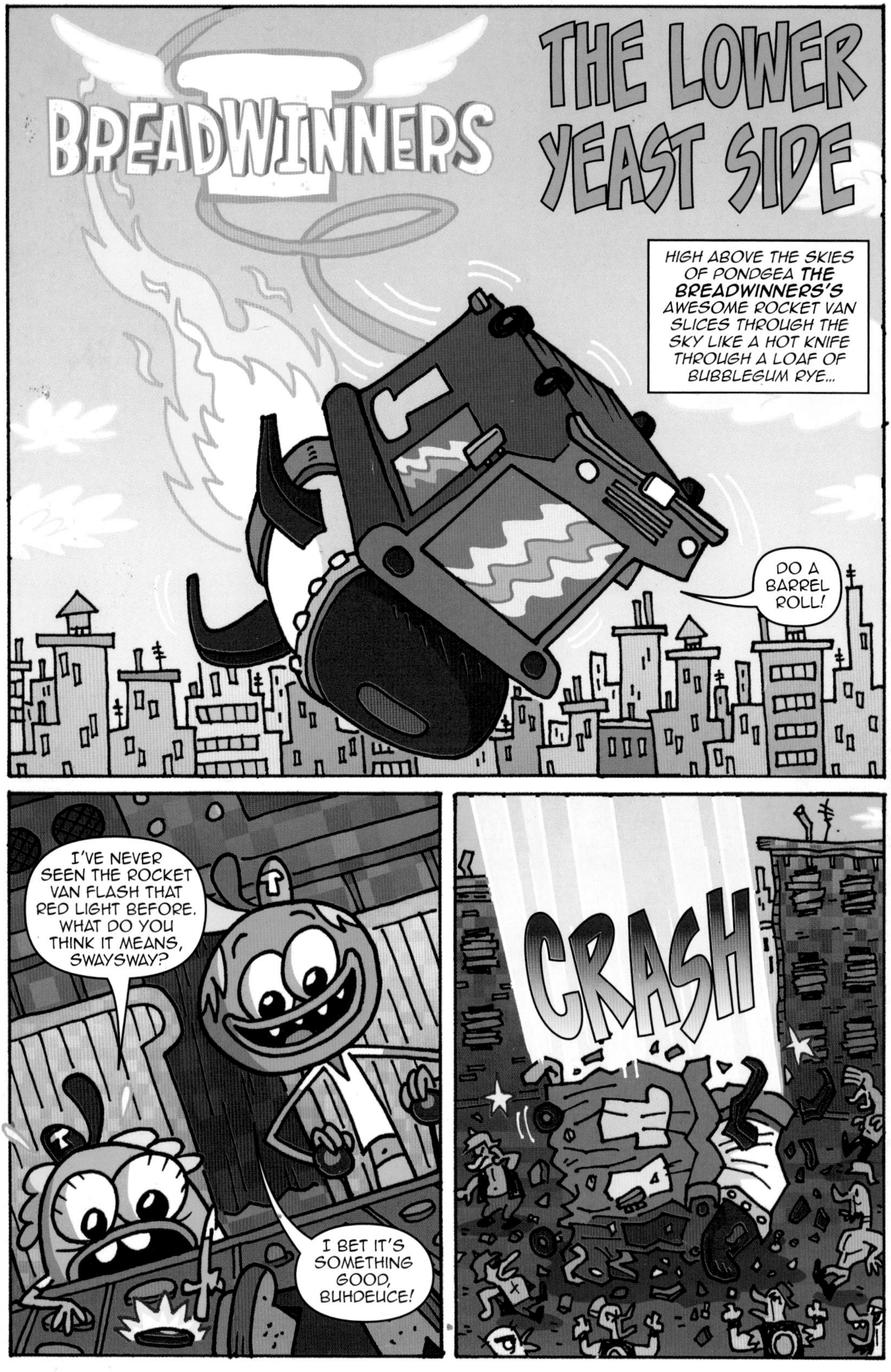
BREADWINNERS
THE LOWER YEAST SIDE
HIGH ABOVE THE SKIES OF PONDGEA **THE BREADWINNERS'S** AWESOME ROCKET VAN SLICES THROUGH THE SKY LIKE A HOT KNIFE THROUGH A LOAF OF BUBBLEGUM RYE...
DO A BARREL ROLL!
I'VE NEVER SEEN THE ROCKET VAN FLASH THAT RED LIGHT BEFORE. WHAT DO YOU THINK IT MEANS, SWAYSWAY?
I BET IT'S SOMETHING GOOD, BUHDEUCE!
CRASH

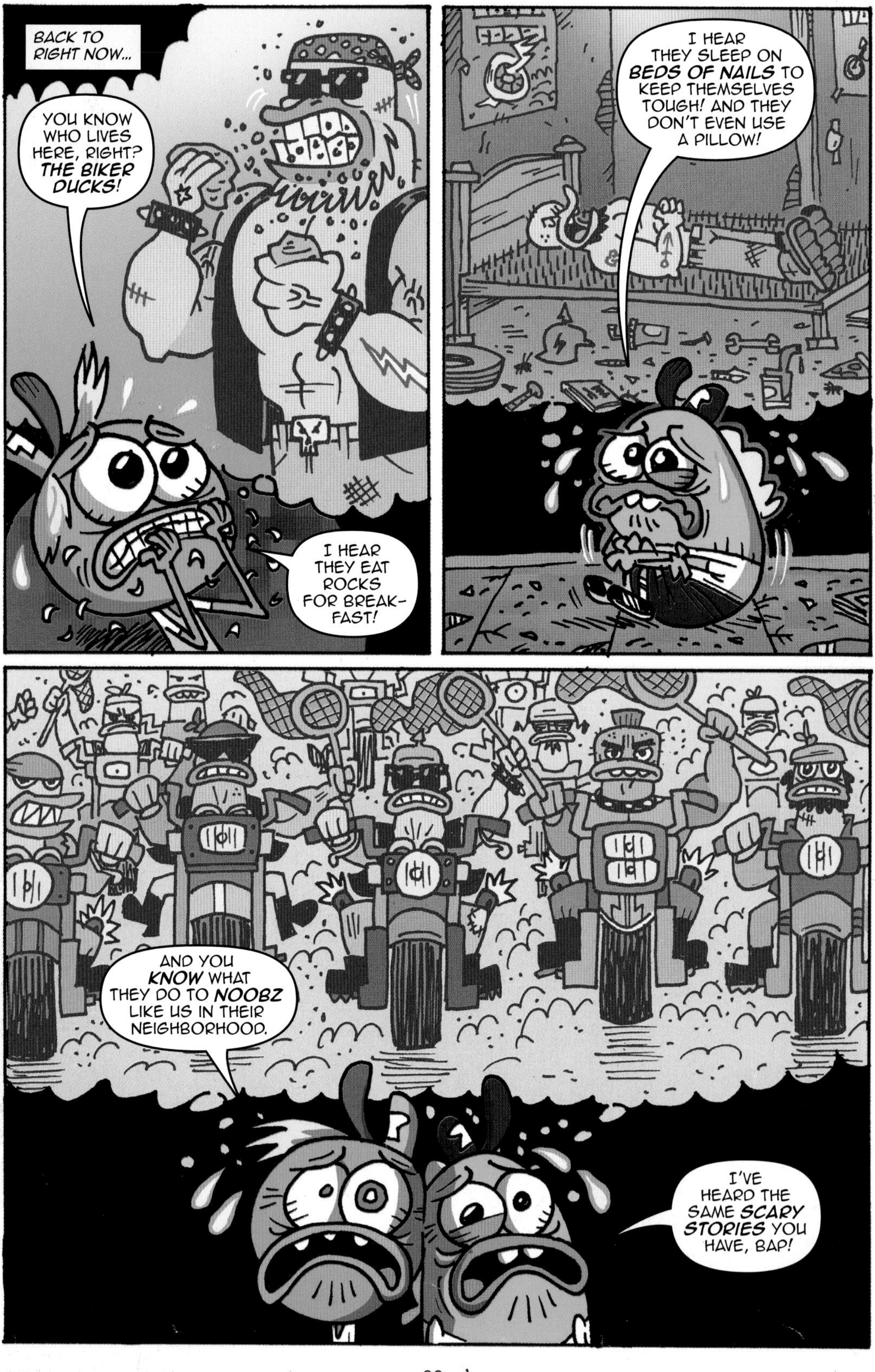
BACK TO RIGHT NOW...
YOU KNOW WHO LIVES HERE, RIGHT? THE BIKER DUCKS!
I HEAR THEY EAT ROCKS FOR BREAK-FAST!
I HEAR THEY SLEEP ON BEDS OF NAILS TO KEEP THEMSELVES TOUGH! AND THEY DON'T EVEN USE A PILLOW!
AND YOU KNOW WHAT THEY DO TO NOOBZ LIKE US IN THEIR NEIGHBORHOOD.
I'VE HEARD THE SAME SCARY STORIES YOU HAVE, BAP!

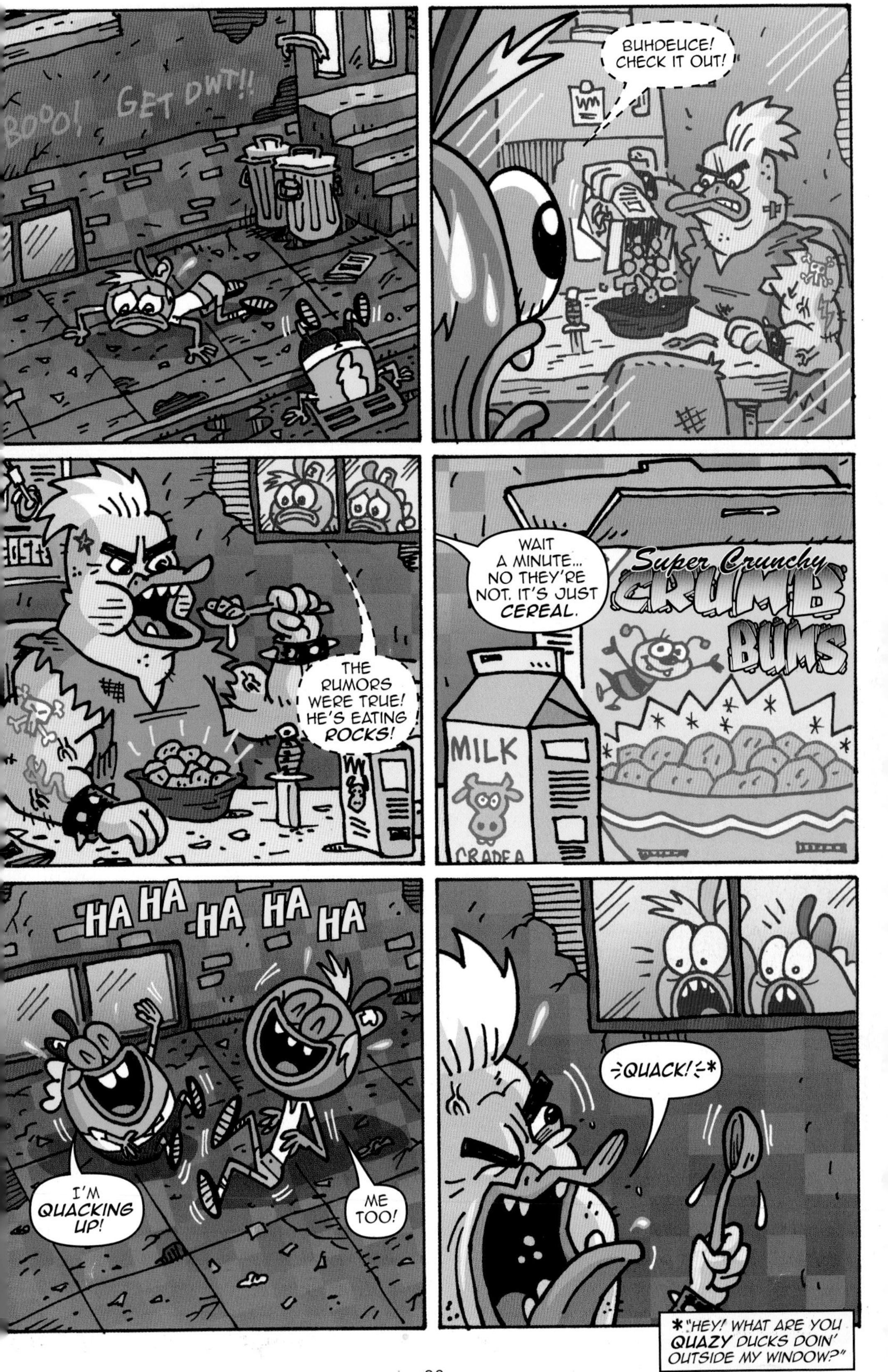
BOOO! GET OWT!!
BUHDEUCE! CHECK IT OUT!
THE RUMORS WERE TRUE! HE'S EATING ROCKS!
WAIT A MINUTE... NO THEY'RE NOT. IT'S JUST CEREAL.
Super Crunchy CRUMB BUMS
MILK
HA HA HA HA HA
I'M QUACKING UP!
ME TOO!
QUACK!*
*"HEY! WHAT ARE YOU QUAZY DUCKS DOIN' OUTSIDE MY WINDOW?"

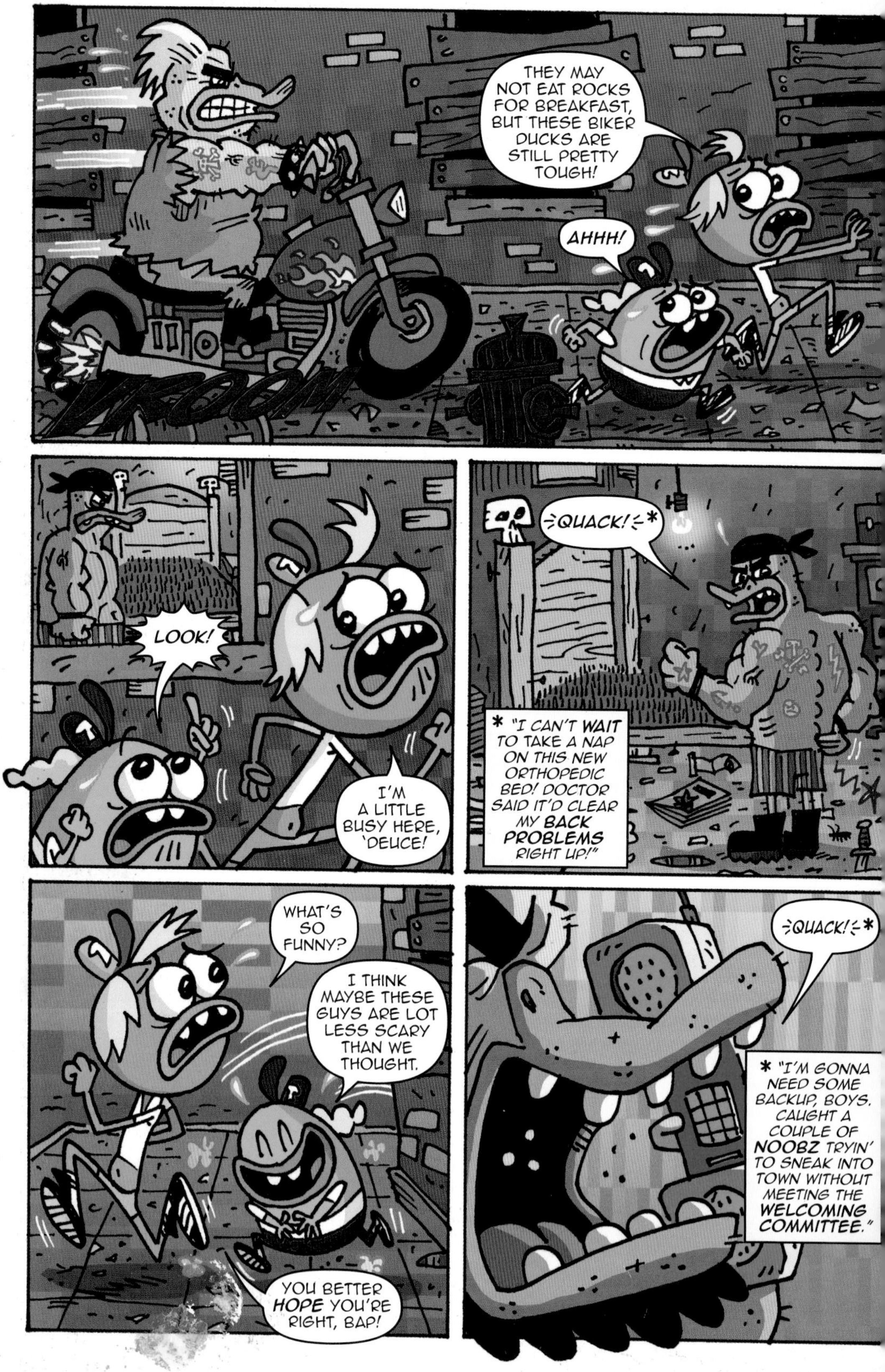
THEY MAY NOT EAT ROCKS FOR BREAKFAST, BUT THESE BIKER DUCKS ARE STILL PRETTY TOUGH!
AHHH!
VROOM
LOOK!
I'M A LITTLE BUSY HERE, 'DEUCE!
-QUACK!-*
* "I CAN'T WAIT TO TAKE A NAP ON THIS NEW ORTHOPEDIC BED! DOCTOR SAID IT'D CLEAR MY BACK PROBLEMS RIGHT UP!"
WHAT'S SO FUNNY?
I THINK MAYBE THESE GUYS ARE LOT LESS SCARY THAN WE THOUGHT.
YOU BETTER HOPE YOU'RE RIGHT, BAP!
-QUACK!-*
* "I'M GONNA NEED SOME BACKUP, BOYS. CAUGHT A COUPLE OF NOOBZ TRYIN' TO SNEAK INTO TOWN WITHOUT MEETING THE WELCOMING COMMITTEE."

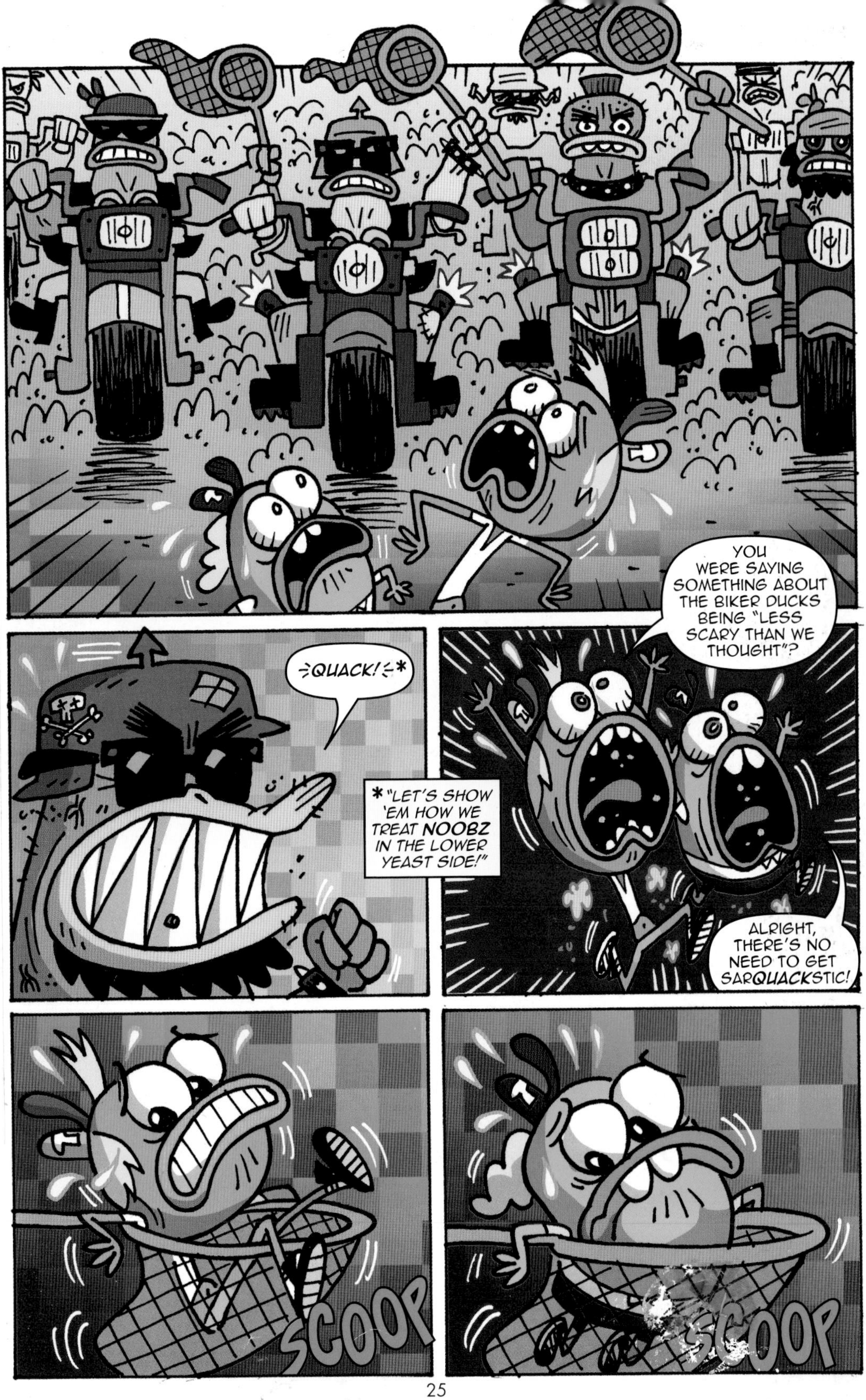
YOU WERE SAYING SOMETHING ABOUT THE BIKER DUCKS BEING "LESS SCARY THAN WE THOUGHT"?
QUACK!*
*"LET'S SHOW 'EM HOW WE TREAT NOOBZ IN THE LOWER YEAST SIDE!"
ALRIGHT, THERE'S NO NEED TO GET SARQUACKSTIC!
SCOOP
SCOOP

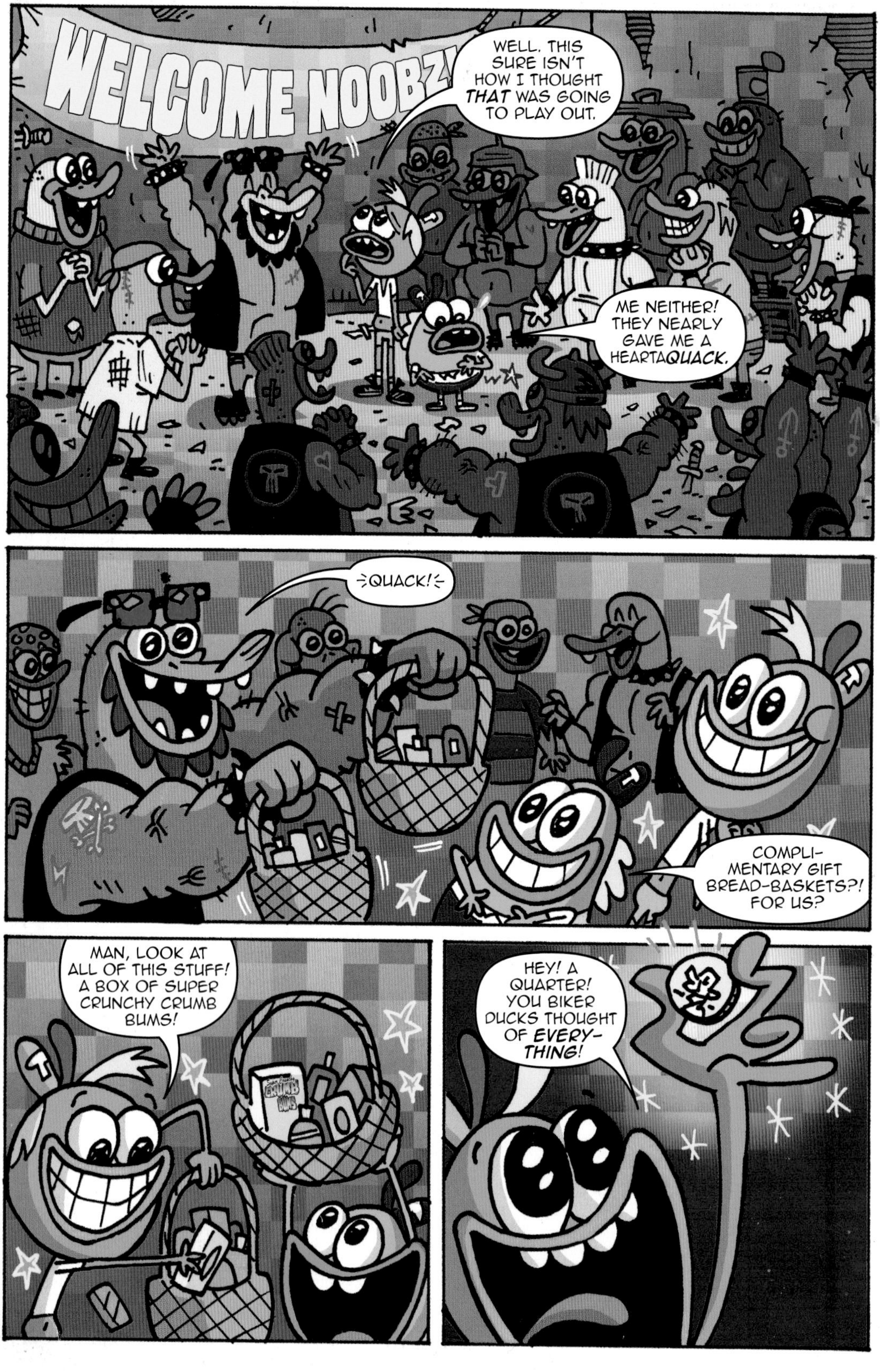
WELCOME NOOBZ!
WELL. THIS SURE ISN'T HOW I THOUGHT THAT WAS GOING TO PLAY OUT.
ME NEITHER! THEY NEARLY GAVE ME A HEARTAQUACK.
QUACK!
COMPLI-MENTARY GIFT BREAD-BASKETS?! FOR US?
MAN, LOOK AT ALL OF THIS STUFF! A BOX OF SUPER CRUNCHY CRUMB BUMS!
HEY! A QUARTER! YOU BIKER DUCKS THOUGHT OF EVERY-THING!

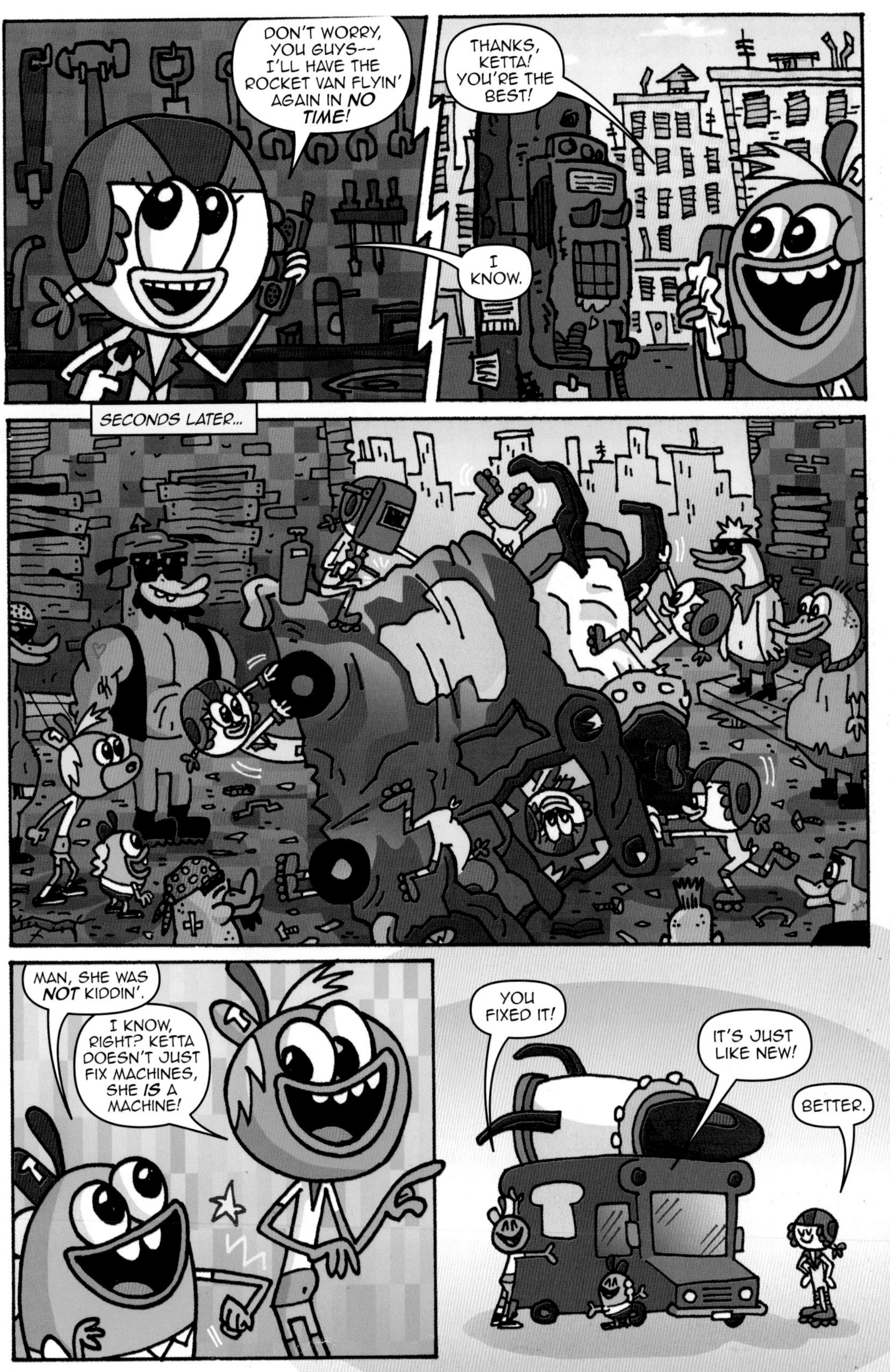
DON'T WORRY, YOU GUYS-- I'LL HAVE THE ROCKET VAN FLYIN' AGAIN IN NO TIME!
THANKS, KETTA! YOU'RE THE BEST!
I KNOW.
SECONDS LATER...
MAN, SHE WAS NOT KIDDIN'.
I KNOW, RIGHT? KETTA DOESN'T JUST FIX MACHINES, SHE IS A MACHINE!
YOU FIXED IT!
IT'S JUST LIKE NEW!
BETTER.

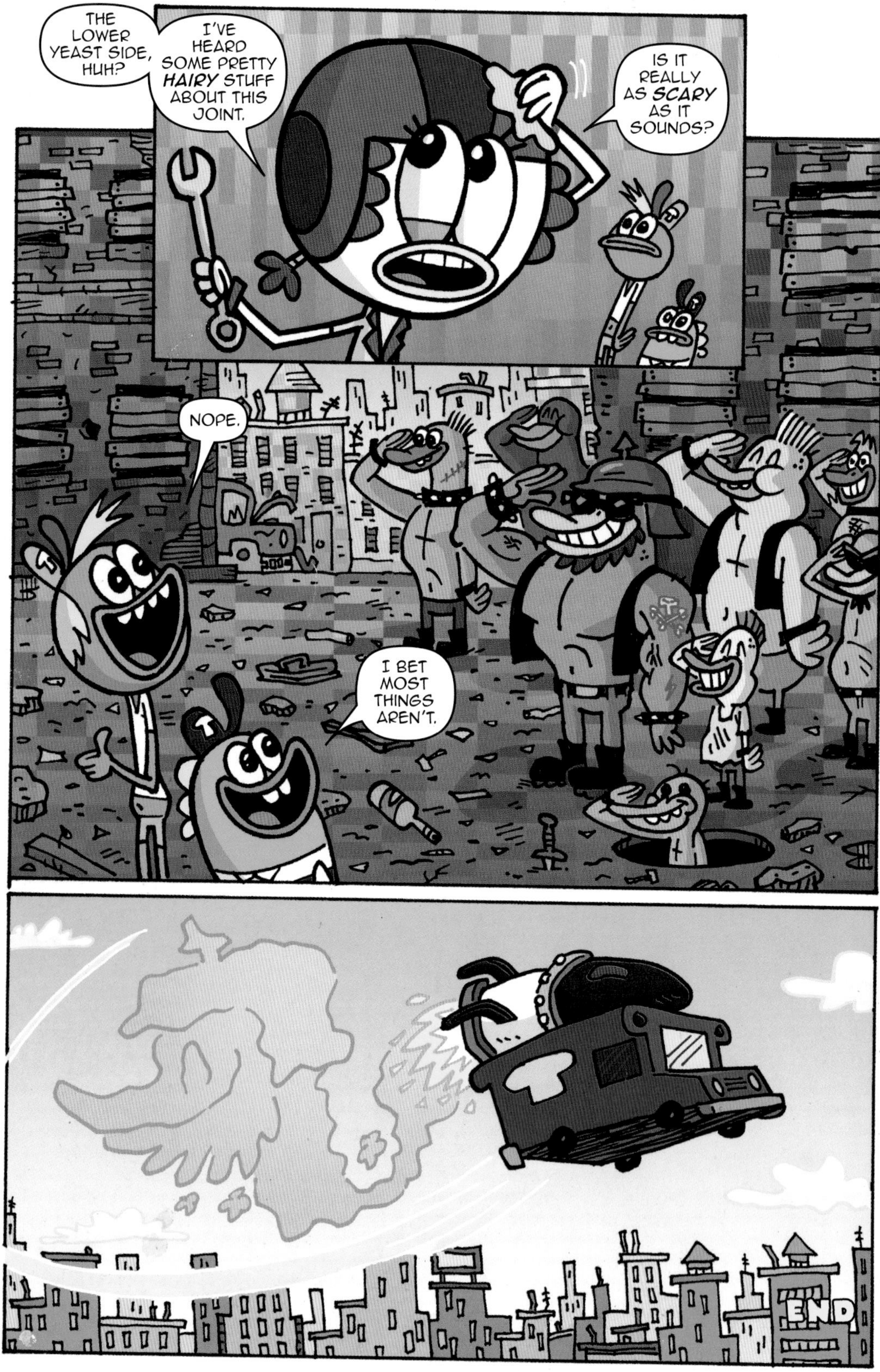
THE LOWER YEAST SIDE, HUH?
I'VE HEARD SOME PRETTY HAIRY STUFF ABOUT THIS JOINT.
IS IT REALLY AS SCARY AS IT SOUNDS?
NOPE.
I BET MOST THINGS AREN'T.
END

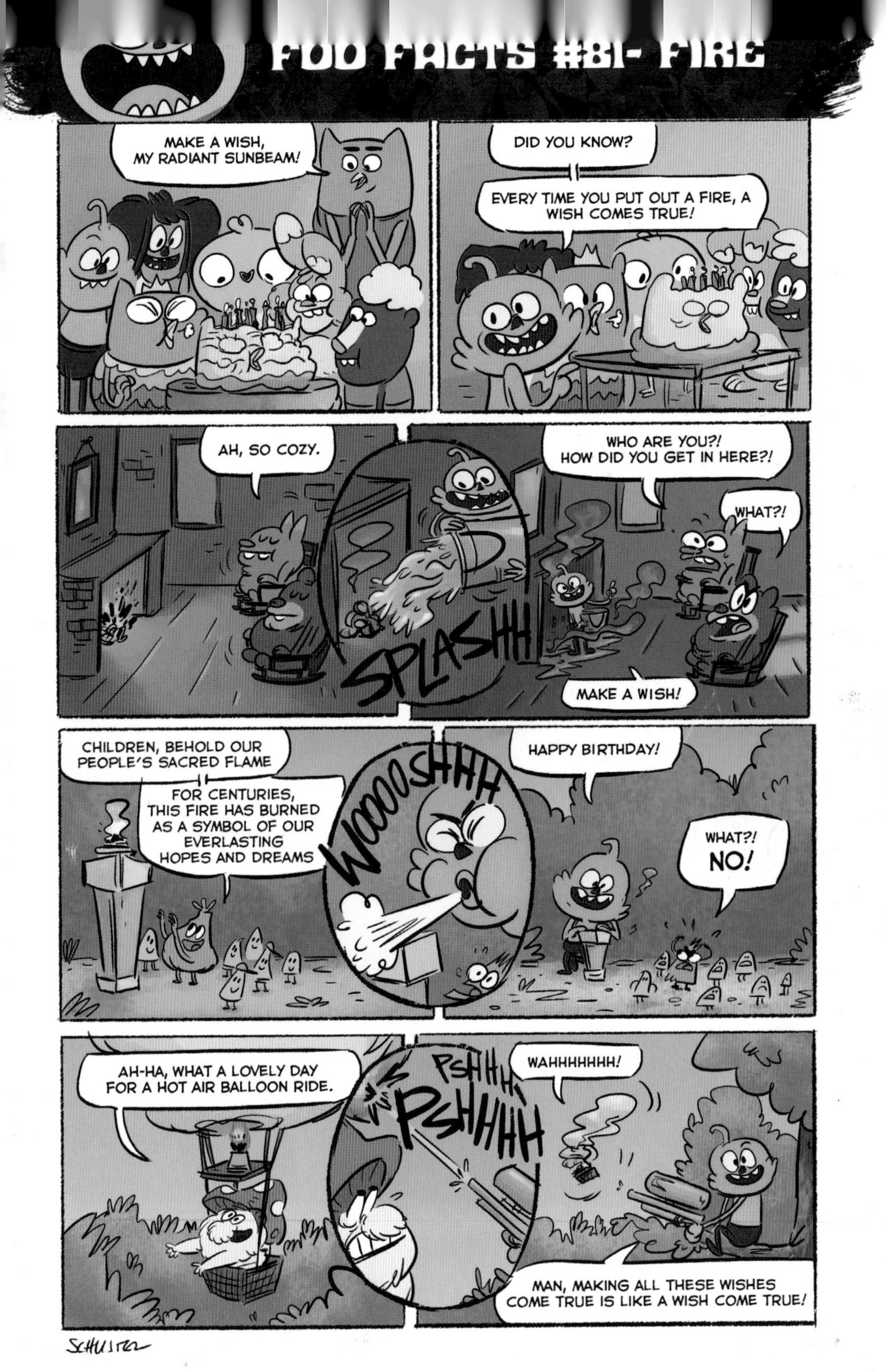
FOO FACTS #81- FIRE
MAKE A WISH, MY RADIANT SUNBEAM!
DID YOU KNOW?
EVERY TIME YOU PUT OUT A FIRE, A WISH COMES TRUE!
AH, SO COZY.
WHO ARE YOU?! HOW DID YOU GET IN HERE?!
WHAT?!
SPLASHHH
MAKE A WISH!
CHILDREN, BEHOLD OUR PEOPLE'S SACRED FLAME
FOR CENTURIES, THIS FIRE HAS BURNED AS A SYMBOL OF OUR EVERLASTING HOPES AND DREAMS
WOOOOSHHH
HAPPY BIRTHDAY!
WHAT?! NO!
AH-HA, WHAT A LOVELY DAY FOR A HOT AIR BALLOON RIDE.
PSHHH, PSHHHH
WAHHHHHHH!
MAN, MAKING ALL THESE WISHES COME TRUE IS LIKE A WISH COME TRUE!
SCHUITEZ

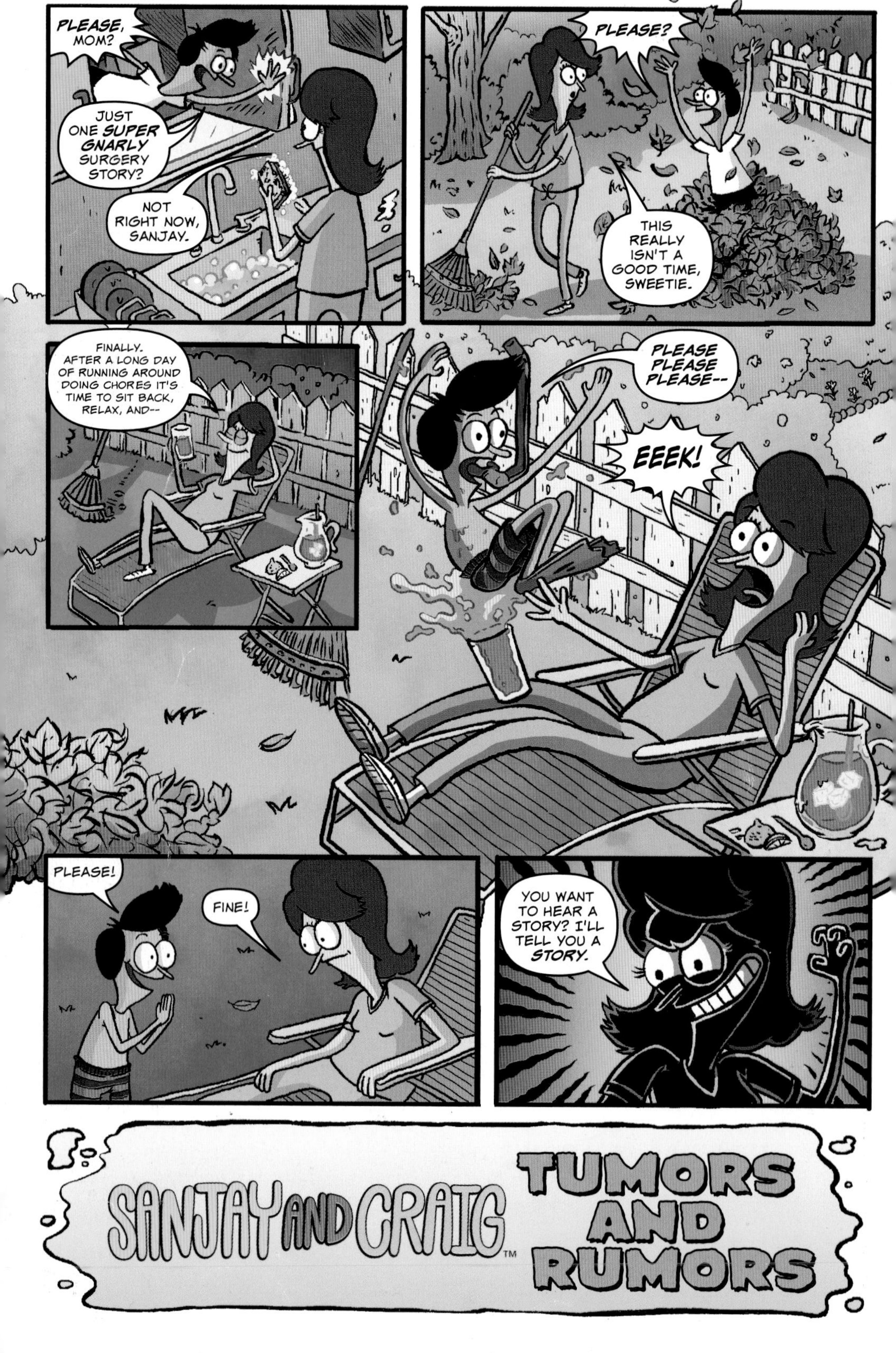
PLEASE, MOM?
JUST ONE SUPER GNARLY SURGERY STORY?
NOT RIGHT NOW, SANJAY.
PLEASE?
THIS REALLY ISN'T A GOOD TIME, SWEETIE.
FINALLY. AFTER A LONG DAY OF RUNNING AROUND DOING CHORES IT'S TIME TO SIT BACK, RELAX, AND--
PLEASE PLEASE PLEASE--
EEEK!
PLEASE!
FINE!
YOU WANT TO HEAR A STORY? I'LL TELL YOU A STORY.
SANJAY AND CRAIG™
TUMORS AND RUMORS

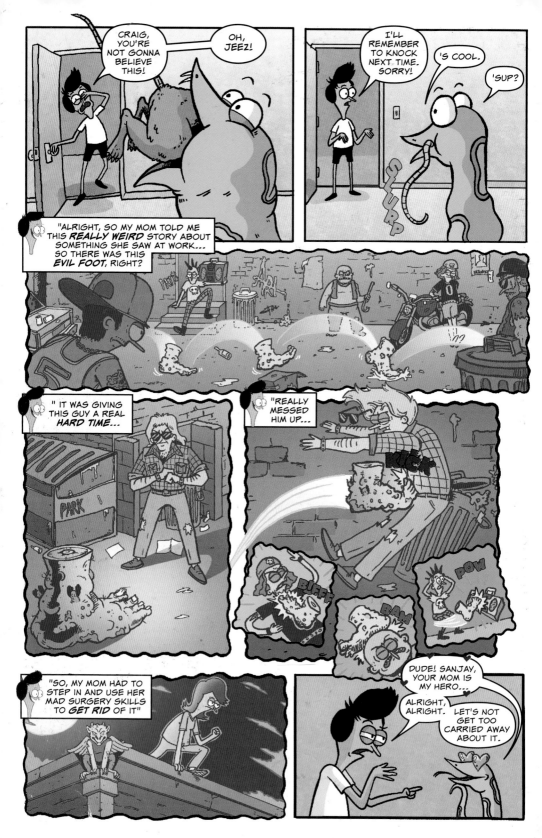

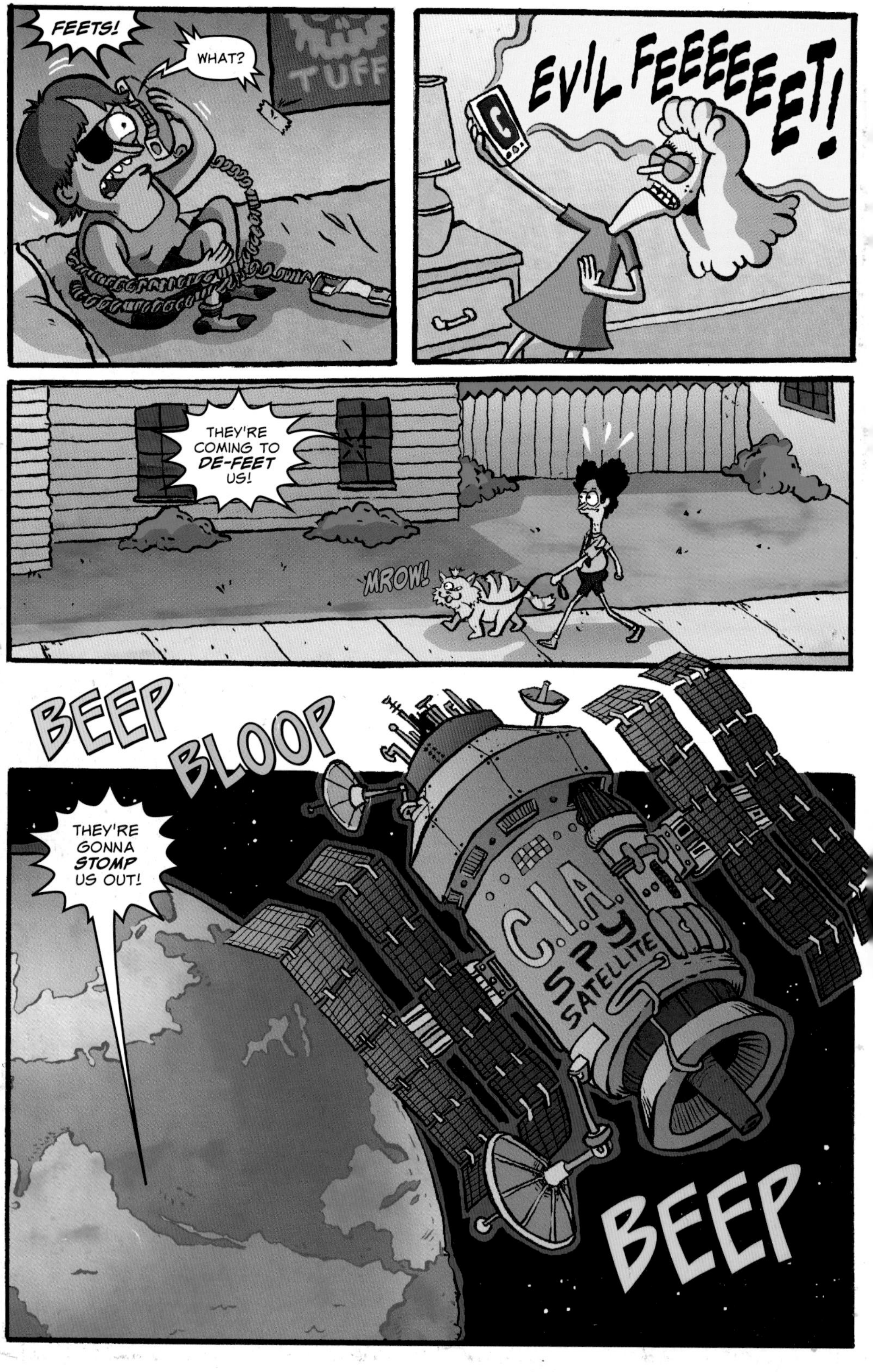
FEETS!
WHAT?
TUFF
EVIL FEEEEEEET!
THEY'RE COMING TO **DE-FEET** US!
MROW!
BEEP
BLOOP
THEY'RE GONNA **STOMP** US OUT!
C.I.A. SPY SATELLITE
BEEP

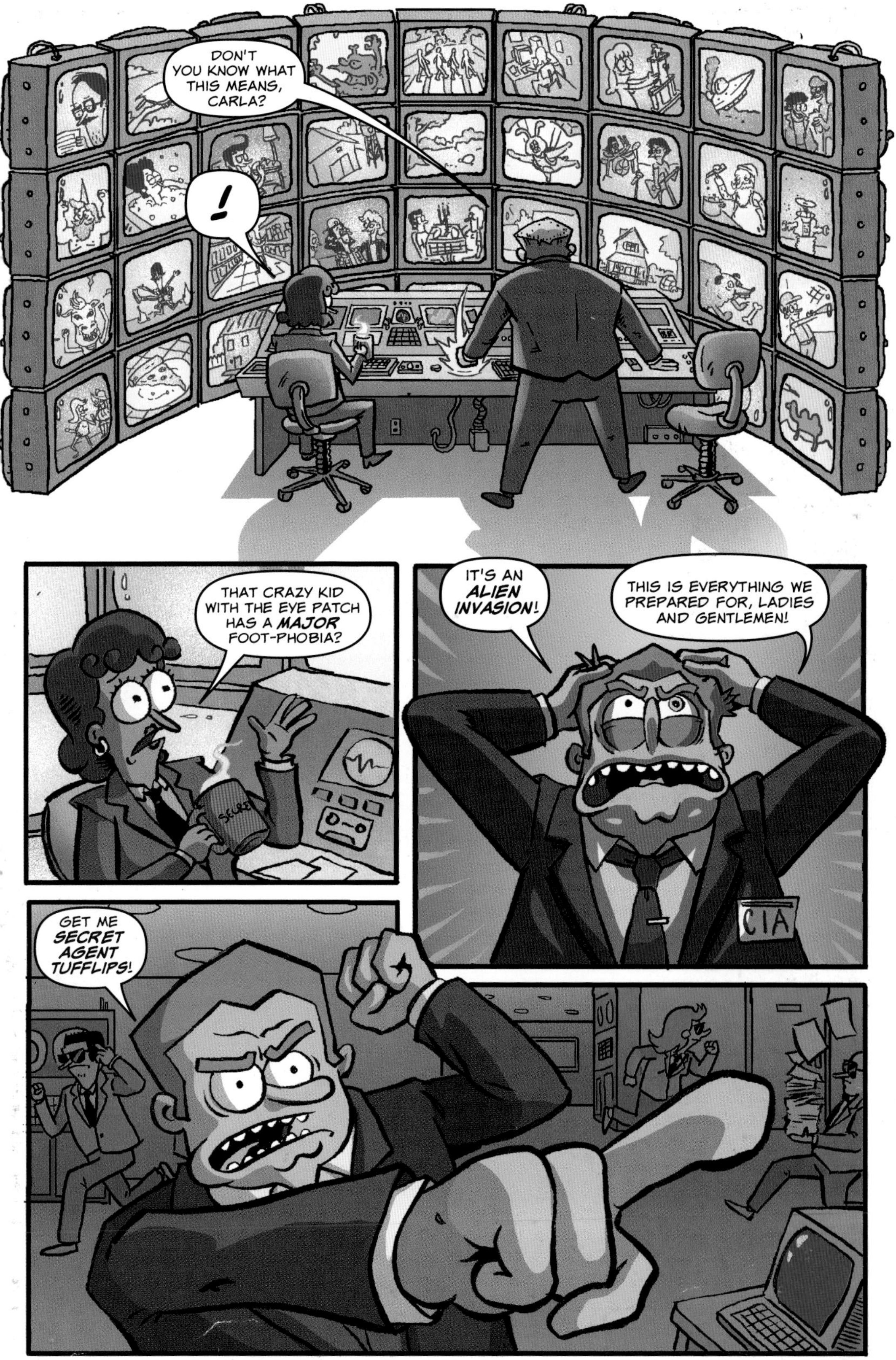
DON'T YOU KNOW WHAT THIS MEANS, CARLA?
!
THAT CRAZY KID WITH THE EYE PATCH HAS A MAJOR FOOT-PHOBIA?
IT'S AN ALIEN INVASION!
THIS IS EVERYTHING WE PREPARED FOR, LADIES AND GENTLEMEN!
CIA
GET ME SECRET AGENT TUFFLIPS!

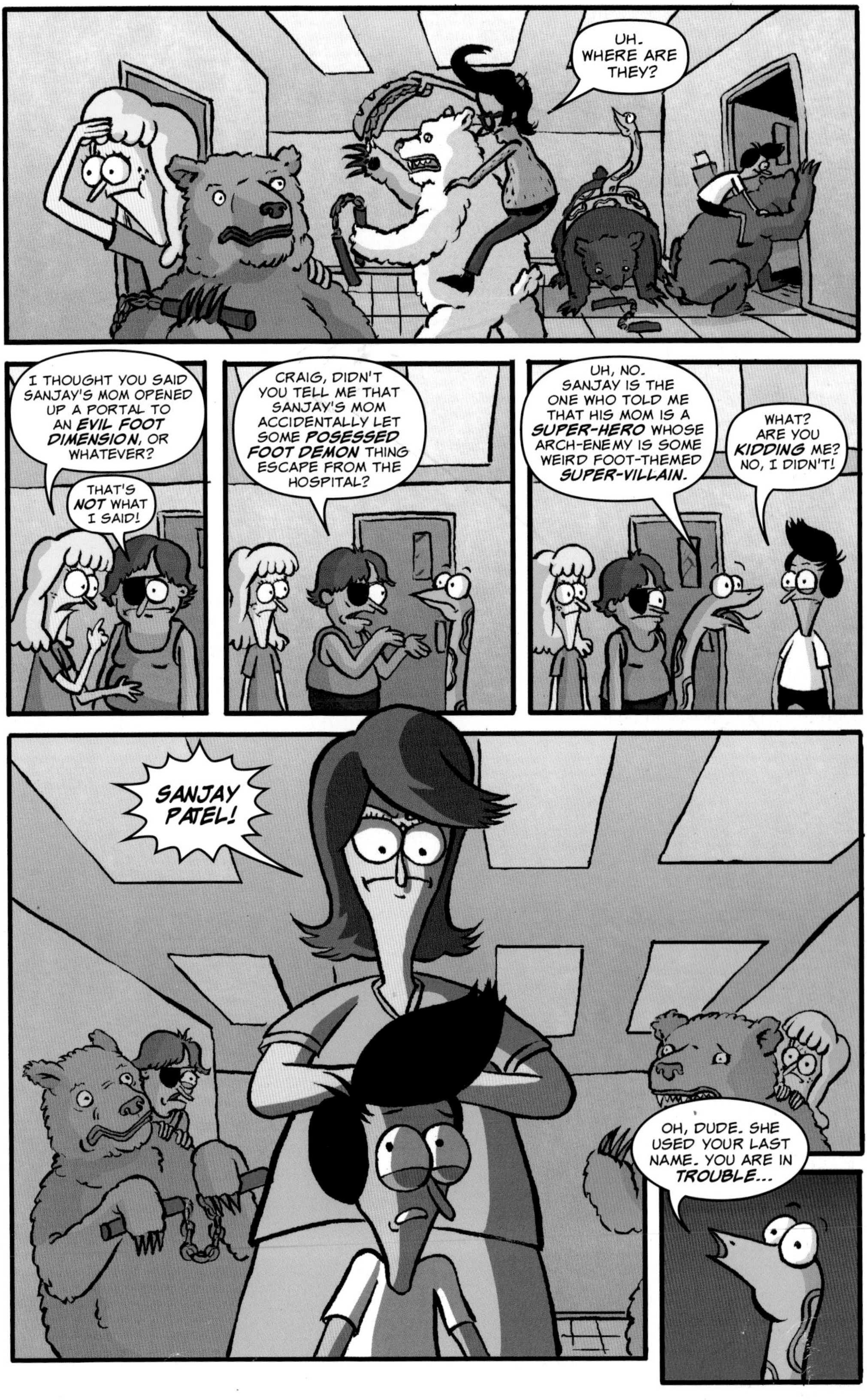
UH. WHERE ARE THEY?
I THOUGHT YOU SAID SANJAY'S MOM OPENED UP A PORTAL TO AN EVIL FOOT DIMENSION, OR WHATEVER?
THAT'S NOT WHAT I SAID!
CRAIG, DIDN'T YOU TELL ME THAT SANJAY'S MOM ACCIDENTALLY LET SOME POSESSED FOOT DEMON THING ESCAPE FROM THE HOSPITAL?
UH, NO. SANJAY IS THE ONE WHO TOLD ME THAT HIS MOM IS A SUPER-HERO WHOSE ARCH-ENEMY IS SOME WEIRD FOOT-THEMED SUPER-VILLAIN.
WHAT? ARE YOU KIDDING ME? NO, I DIDN'T!
SANJAY PATEL!
OH, DUDE. SHE USED YOUR LAST NAME. YOU ARE IN TROUBLE...

38

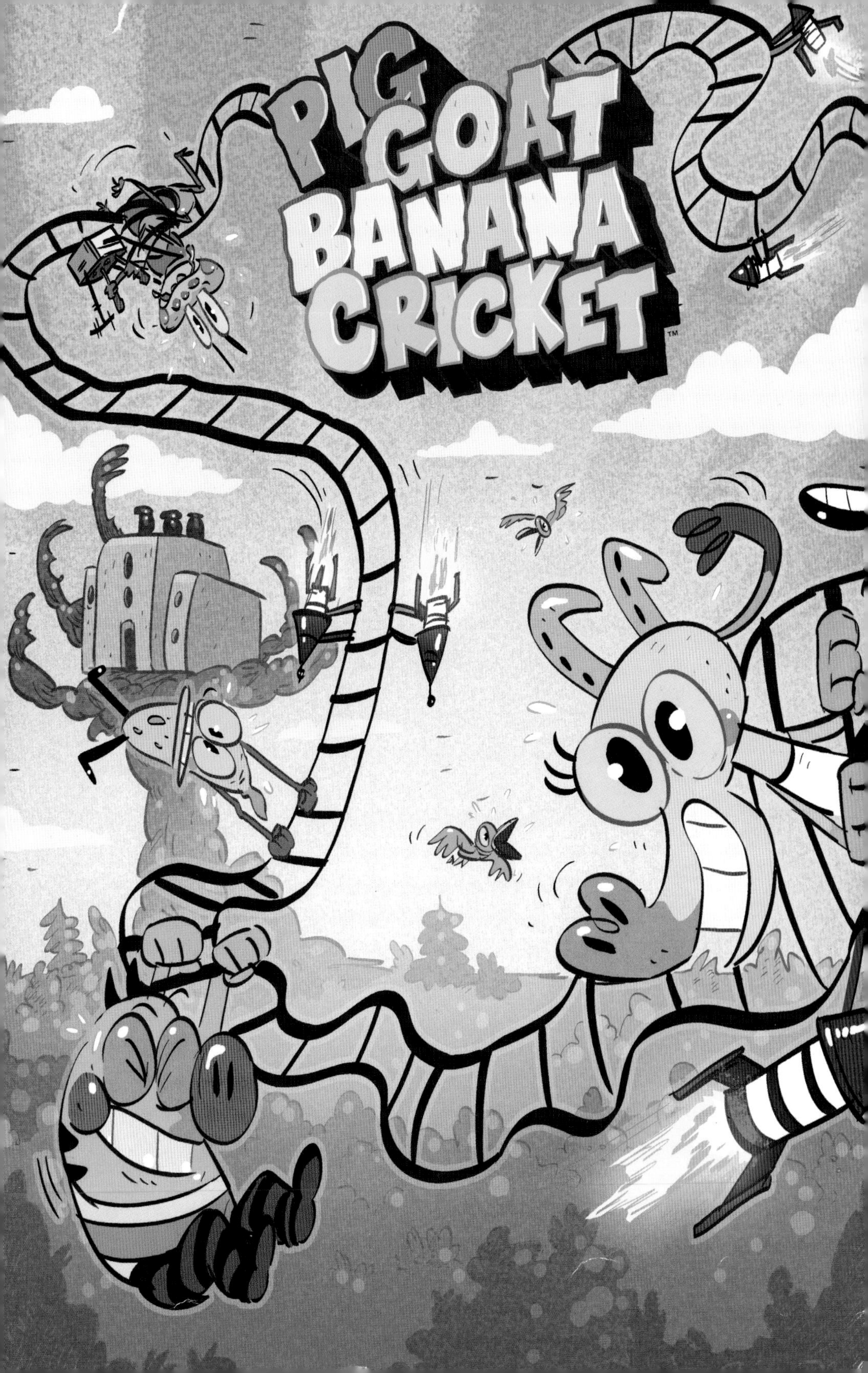
PIG GOAT BANANA CRICKET™

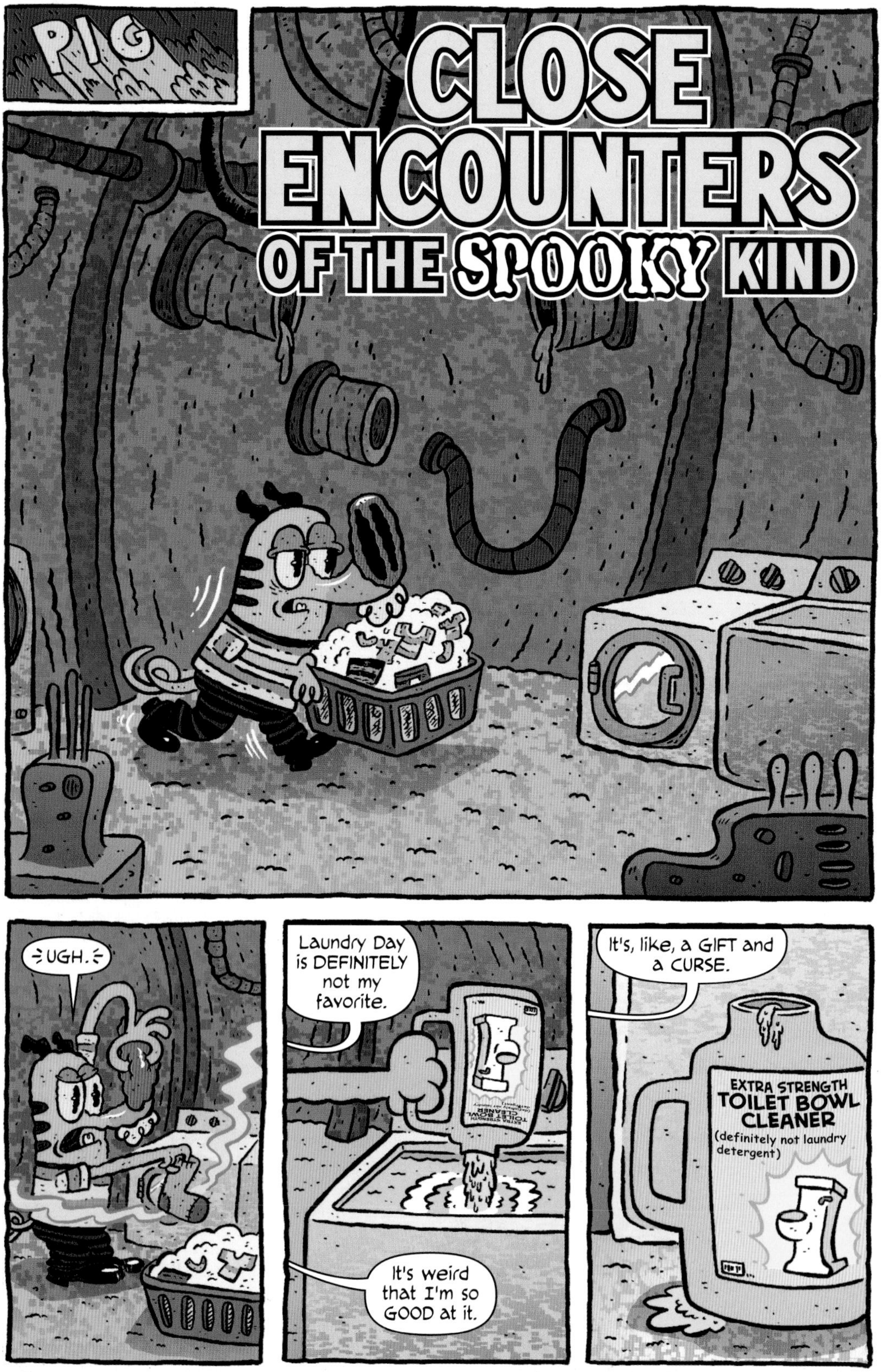
PIG
CLOSE ENCOUNTERS OF THE SPOOKY KIND
UGH.
Laundry Day is DEFINITELY not my favorite.
It's weird that I'm so GOOD at it.
It's, like, a GIFT and a CURSE.
EXTRA STRENGTH
TOILET BOWL CLEANER
(definitely not laundry detergent)

BANANA

Later...

PAT PAT

It was just so SPOOKY.

You really think you saw a ghost?

I know I sound silly. Everybody knows that ghosts aren't REALLY real.

No, dude. I believe you. Ghosts are TOTALLY real.

CHOMP
CHOMP

43

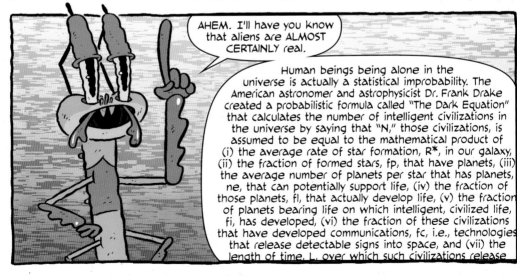

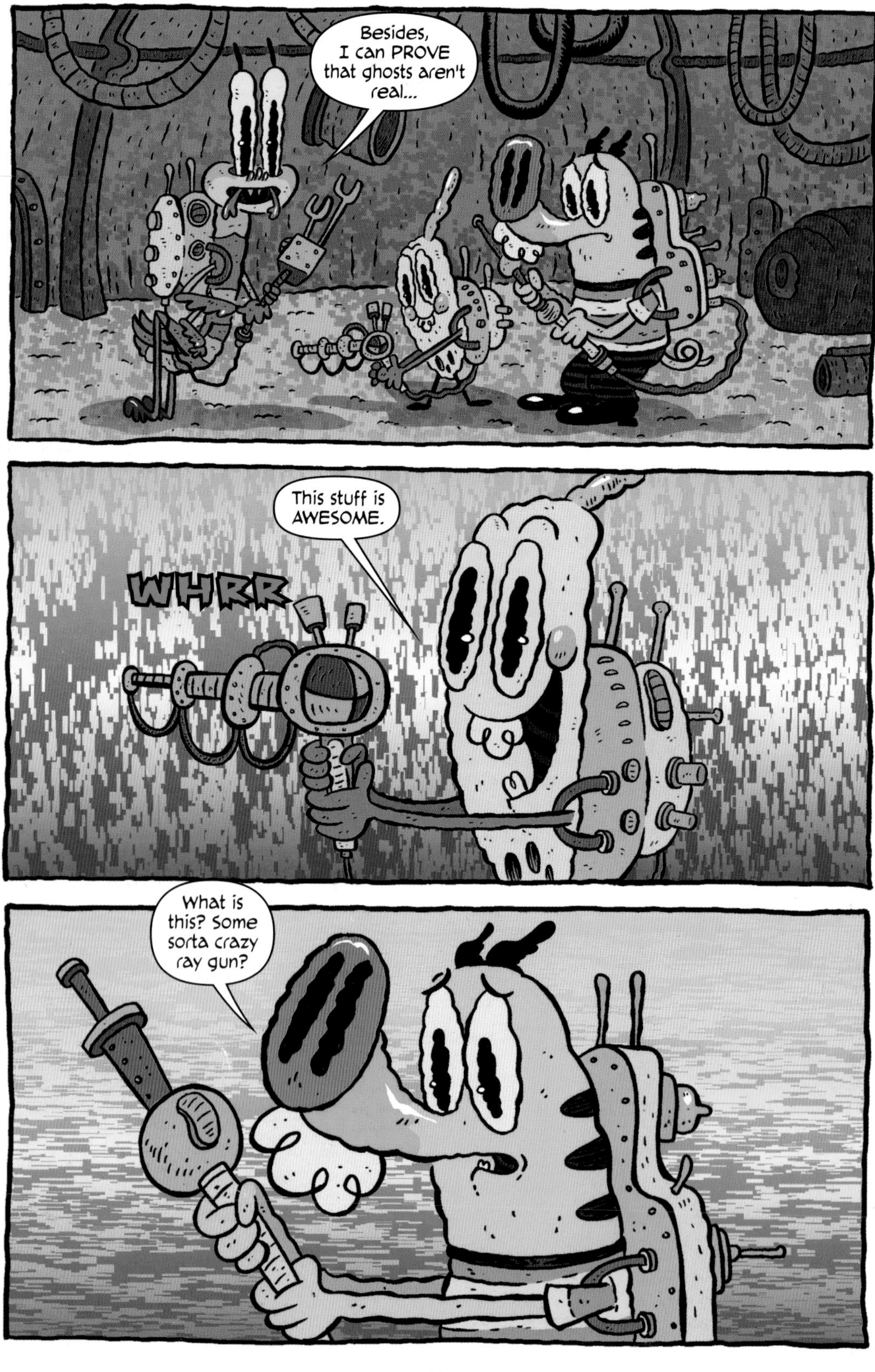
Besides, I can PROVE that ghosts aren't real...
This stuff is AWESOME.
WHRR
What is this? Some sorta crazy ray gun?

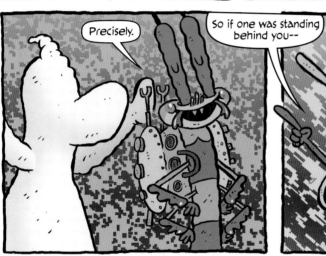

END?

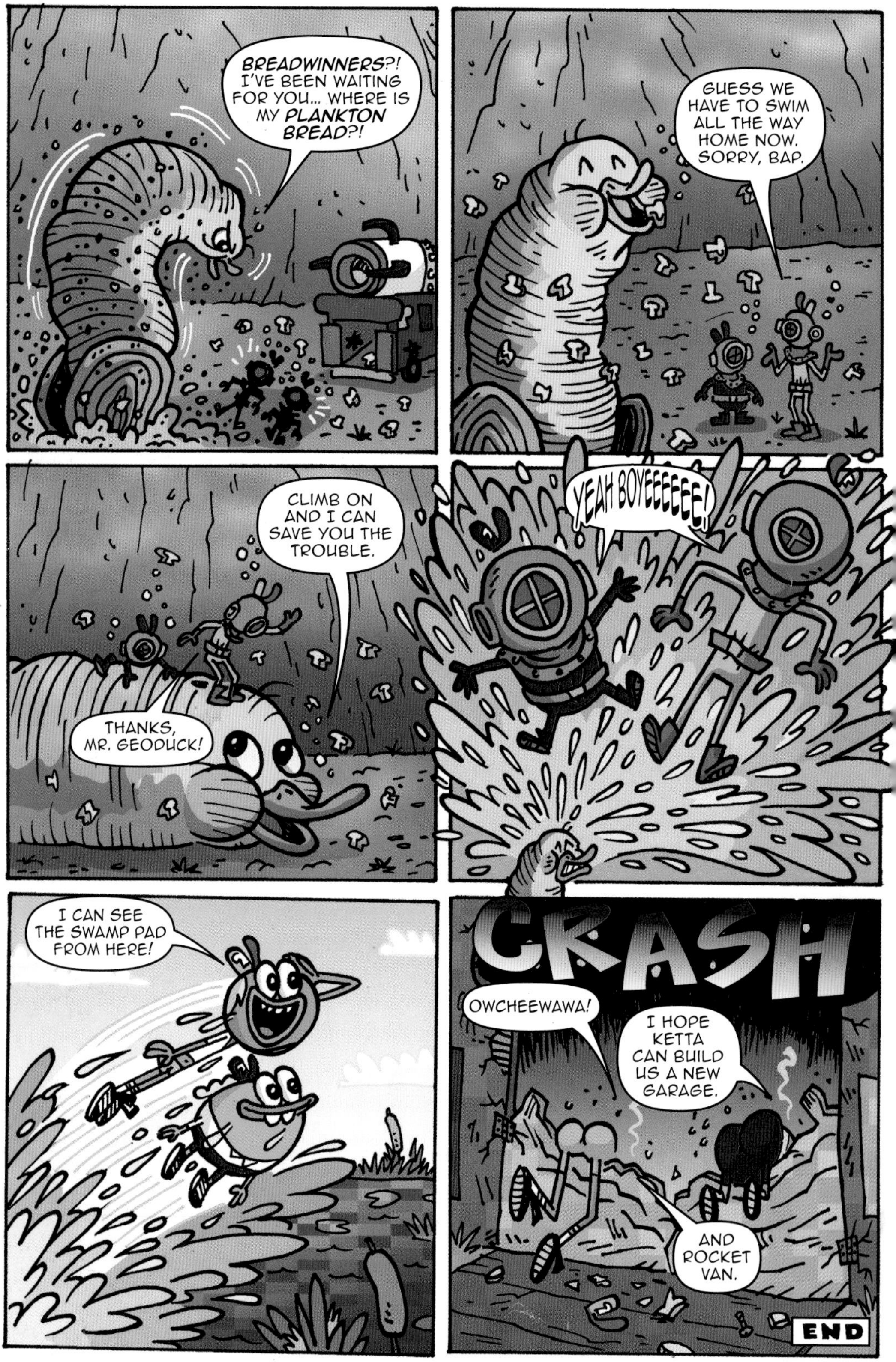
BREADWINNERS?! I'VE BEEN WAITING FOR YOU... WHERE IS MY PLANKTON BREAD?!
GUESS WE HAVE TO SWIM ALL THE WAY HOME NOW. SORRY, BAP.
CLIMB ON AND I CAN SAVE YOU THE TROUBLE.
THANKS, MR. GEODUCK!
YEAH BOYEEEEEE!
I CAN SEE THE SWAMP PAD FROM HERE!
CRASH
OWCHEEWAWA!
I HOPE KETTA CAN BUILD US A NEW GARAGE.
AND ROCKET VAN.
END

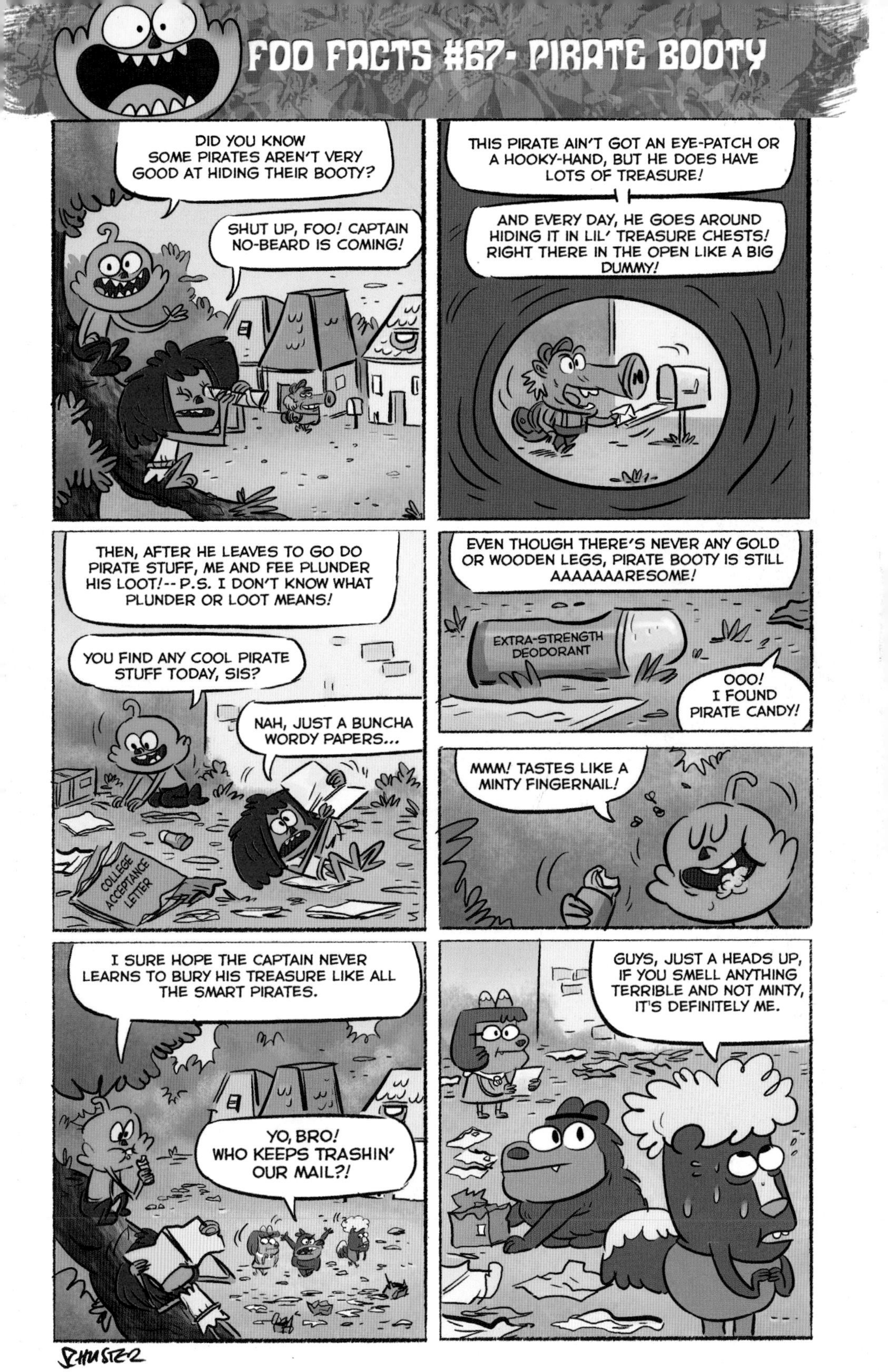
FOO FACTS #67- PIRATE BOOTY
DID YOU KNOW SOME PIRATES AREN'T VERY GOOD AT HIDING THEIR BOOTY?
SHUT UP, FOO! CAPTAIN NO-BEARD IS COMING!
THIS PIRATE AIN'T GOT AN EYE-PATCH OR A HOOKY-HAND, BUT HE DOES HAVE LOTS OF TREASURE!
AND EVERY DAY, HE GOES AROUND HIDING IT IN LIL' TREASURE CHESTS! RIGHT THERE IN THE OPEN LIKE A BIG DUMMY!
THEN, AFTER HE LEAVES TO GO DO PIRATE STUFF, ME AND FEE PLUNDER HIS LOOT!-- P.S. I DON'T KNOW WHAT PLUNDER OR LOOT MEANS!
YOU FIND ANY COOL PIRATE STUFF TODAY, SIS?
NAH, JUST A BUNCHA WORDY PAPERS...
COLLEGE ACCEPTANCE LETTER
EVEN THOUGH THERE'S NEVER ANY GOLD OR WOODEN LEGS, PIRATE BOOTY IS STILL AAAAAAARESOME!
EXTRA-STRENGTH DEODORANT
OOO! I FOUND PIRATE CANDY!
MMM! TASTES LIKE A MINTY FINGERNAIL!
I SURE HOPE THE CAPTAIN NEVER LEARNS TO BURY HIS TREASURE LIKE ALL THE SMART PIRATES.
YO, BRO! WHO KEEPS TRASHIN' OUR MAIL?!
GUYS, JUST A HEADS UP, IF YOU SMELL ANYTHING TERRIBLE AND NOT MINTY, IT'S DEFINITELY ME.
SCHUSTER

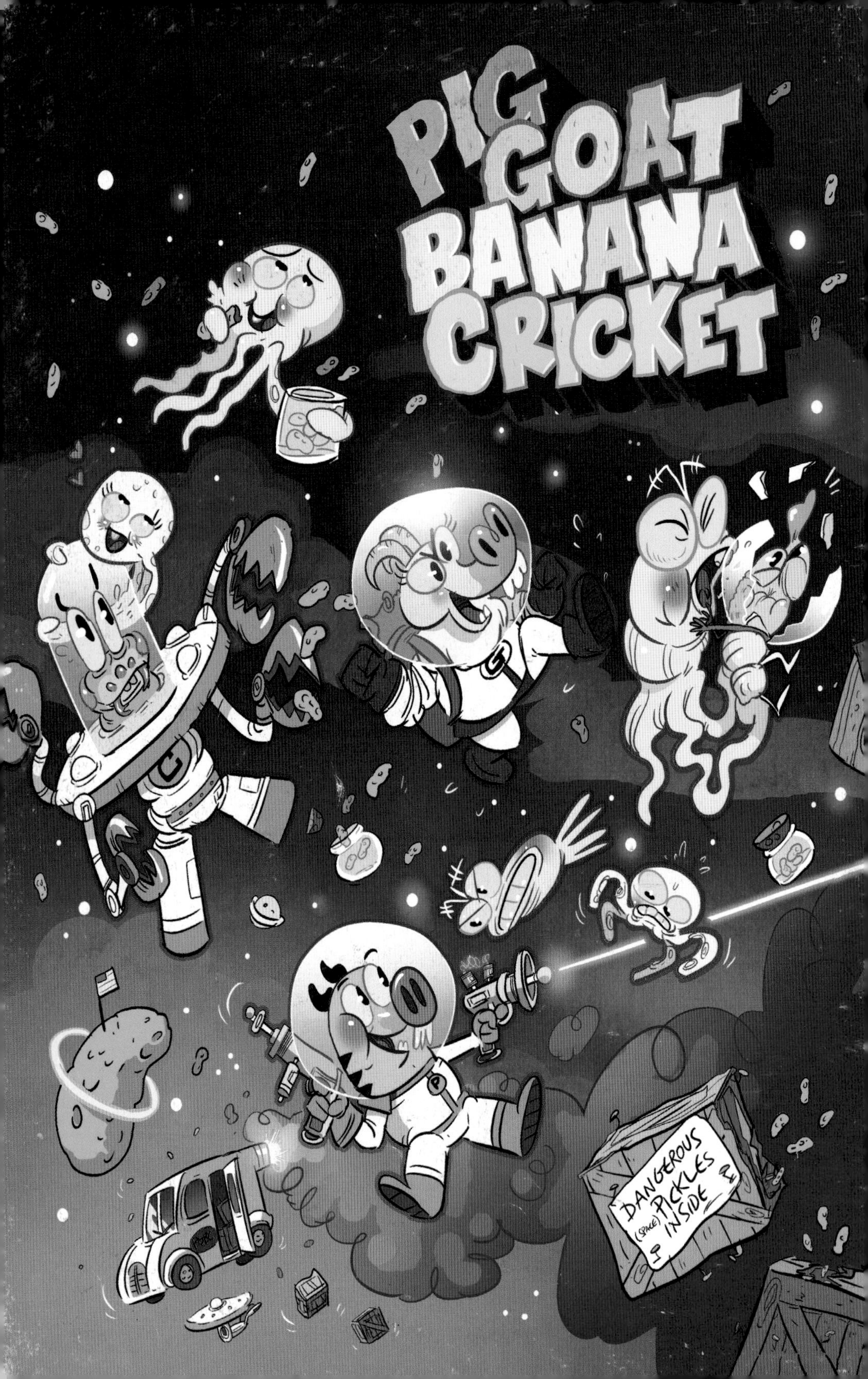
PIG GOAT BANANA CRICKET
DANGEROUS (SPACE) PICKLES INSIDE

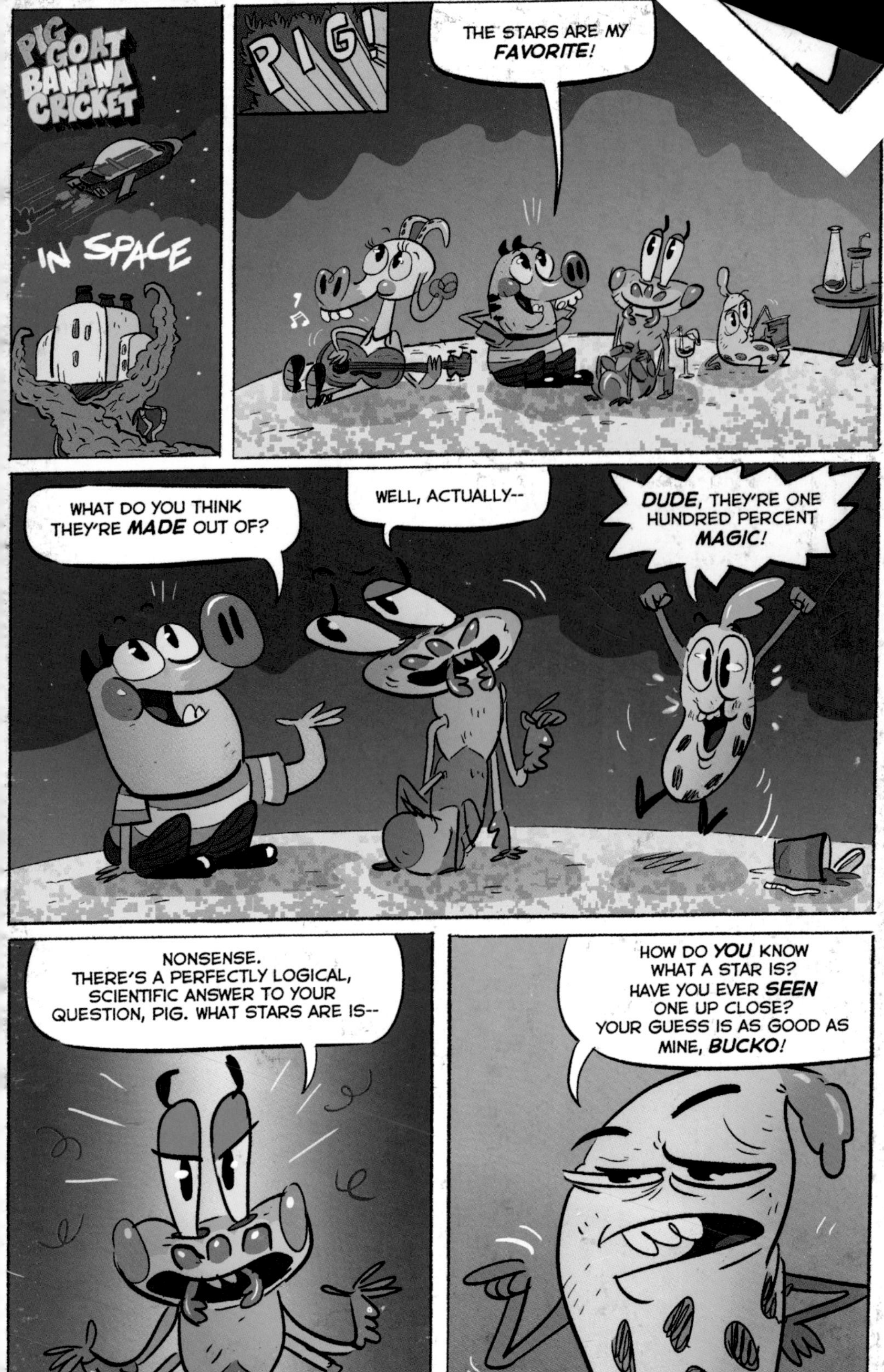
PIG GOAT BANANA CRICKET
IN SPACE
PIG!
THE STARS ARE MY FAVORITE!
WHAT DO YOU THINK THEY'RE MADE OUT OF?
WELL, ACTUALLY--
DUDE, THEY'RE ONE HUNDRED PERCENT MAGIC!
NONSENSE. THERE'S A PERFECTLY LOGICAL, SCIENTIFIC ANSWER TO YOUR QUESTION, PIG. WHAT STARS ARE IS--
HOW DO YOU KNOW WHAT A STAR IS? HAVE YOU EVER SEEN ONE UP CLOSE? YOUR GUESS IS AS GOOD AS MINE, BUCKO!

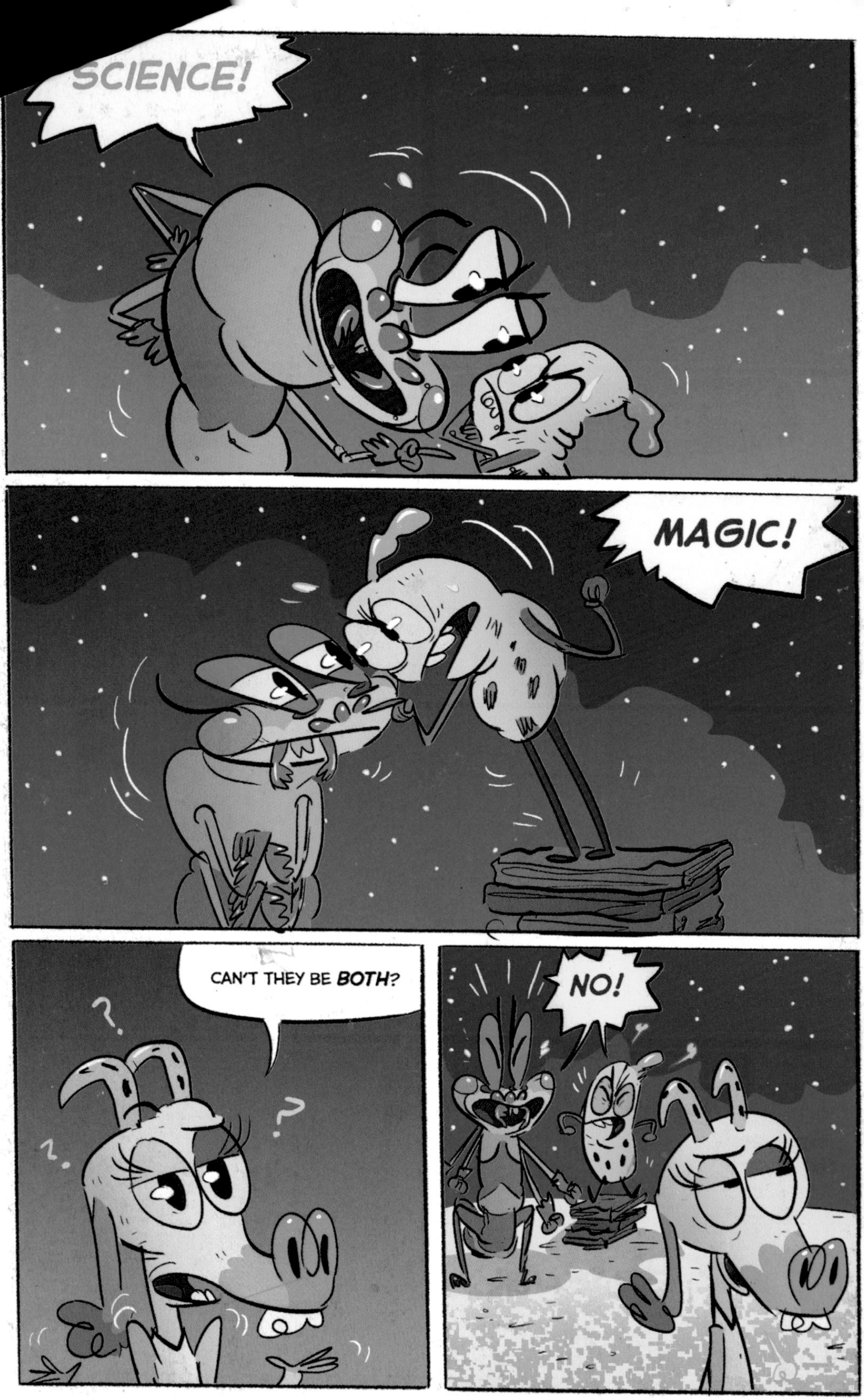
SCIENCE!
MAGIC!
CAN'T THEY BE BOTH?
NO!

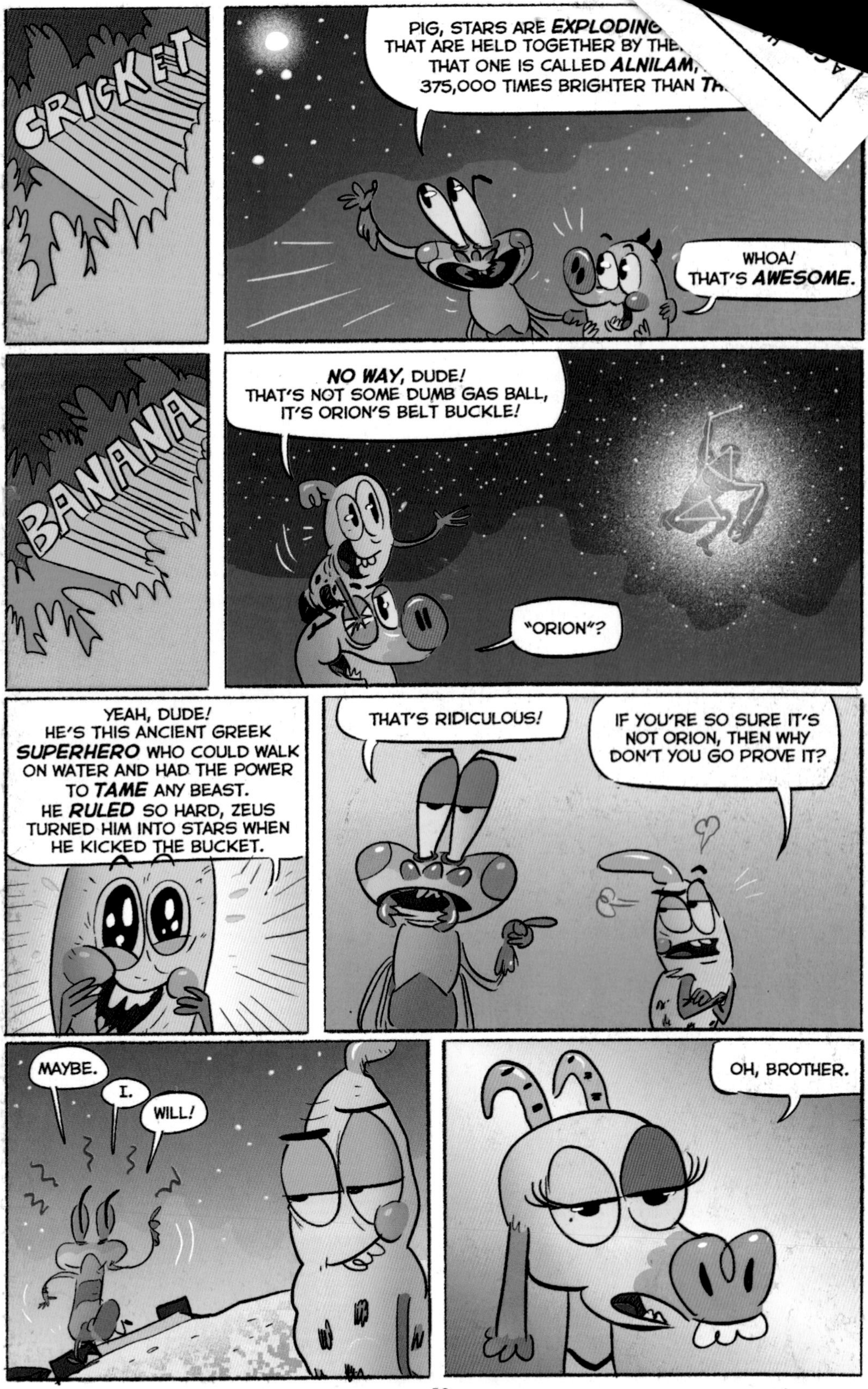
CRICKET
PIG, STARS ARE EXPLODING
THAT ARE HELD TOGETHER BY THE
THAT ONE IS CALLED ALNILAM,
375,000 TIMES BRIGHTER THAN
WHOA! THAT'S AWESOME.
BANANA
NO WAY, DUDE! THAT'S NOT SOME DUMB GAS BALL, IT'S ORION'S BELT BUCKLE!
"ORION"?
YEAH, DUDE! HE'S THIS ANCIENT GREEK SUPERHERO WHO COULD WALK ON WATER AND HAD THE POWER TO TAME ANY BEAST. HE RULED SO HARD, ZEUS TURNED HIM INTO STARS WHEN HE KICKED THE BUCKET.
THAT'S RIDICULOUS!
IF YOU'RE SO SURE IT'S NOT ORION, THEN WHY DON'T YOU GO PROVE IT?
MAYBE.
I.
WILL!
OH, BROTHER.

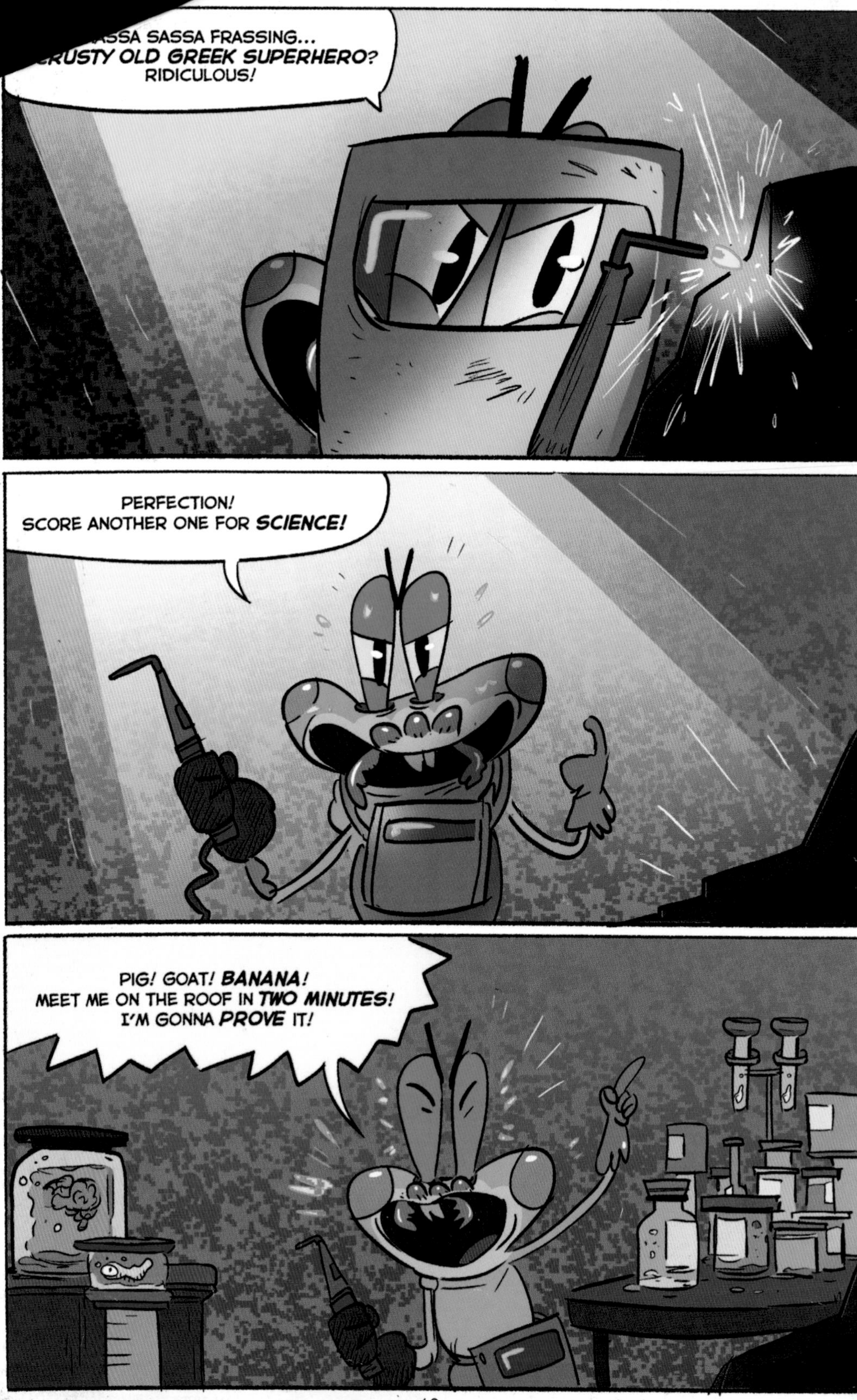
ASSA SASSA FRASSING...
RUSTY OLD GREEK SUPERHERO?
RIDICULOUS!
PERFECTION!
SCORE ANOTHER ONE FOR SCIENCE!
PIG! GOAT! BANANA!
MEET ME ON THE ROOF IN TWO MINUTES!
I'M GONNA PROVE IT!

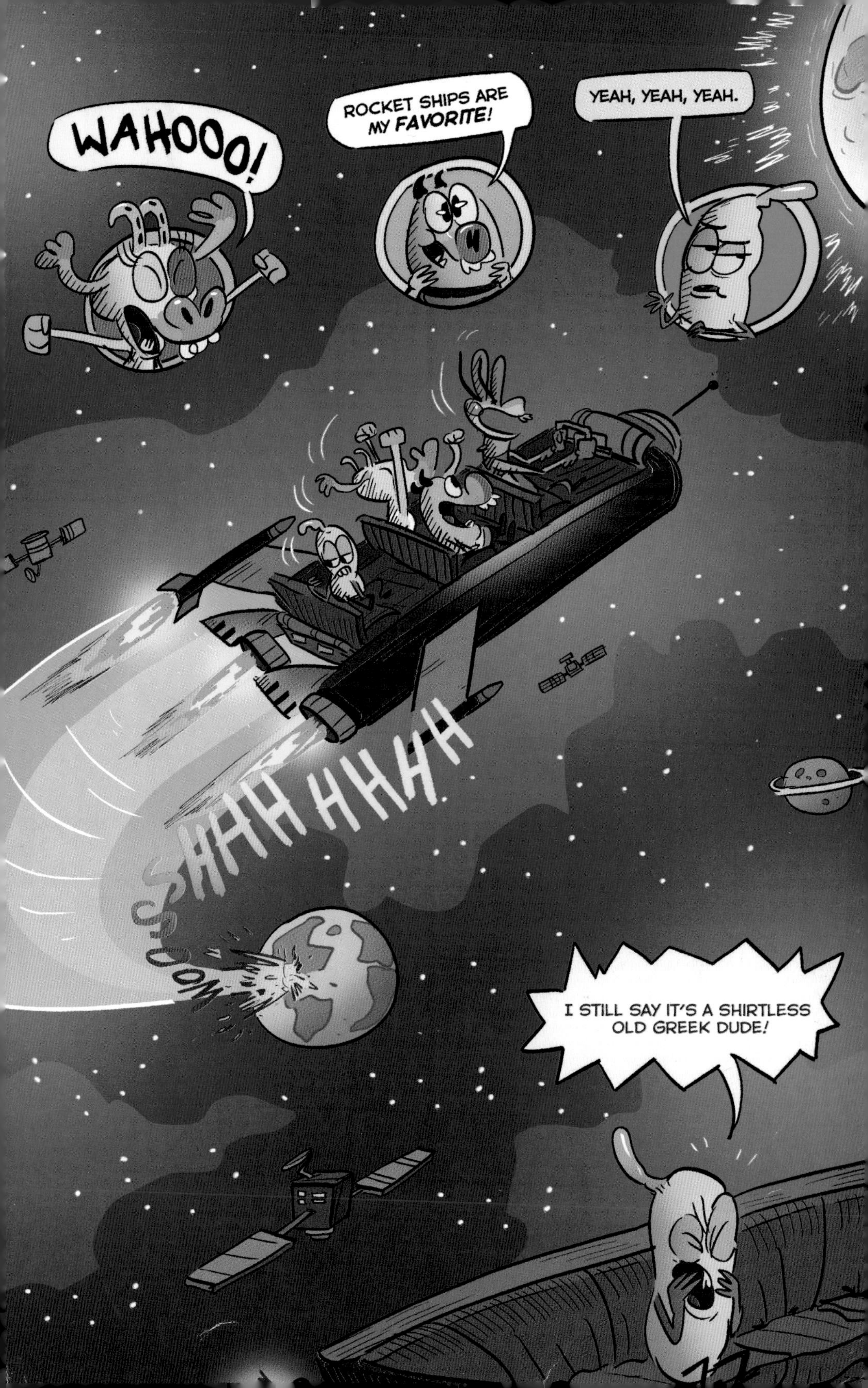
WAHOOO!
ROCKET SHIPS ARE MY FAVORITE!
YEAH, YEAH, YEAH.
SHHHHHHH
SWOOM
I STILL SAY IT'S A SHIRTLESS OLD GREEK DUDE!

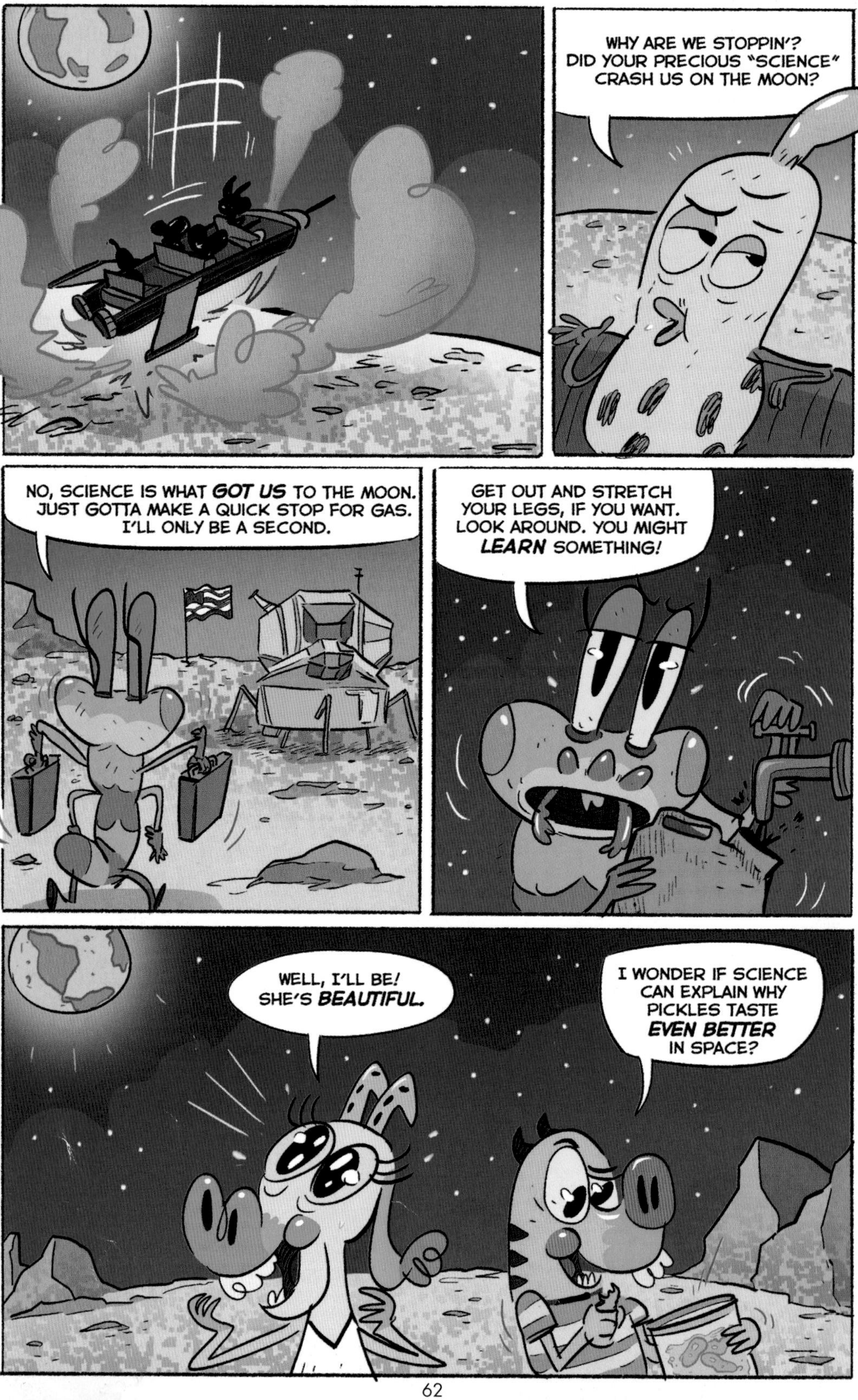
WHY ARE WE STOPPIN'? DID YOUR PRECIOUS "SCIENCE" CRASH US ON THE MOON?
NO, SCIENCE IS WHAT GOT US TO THE MOON. JUST GOTTA MAKE A QUICK STOP FOR GAS. I'LL ONLY BE A SECOND.
GET OUT AND STRETCH YOUR LEGS, IF YOU WANT. LOOK AROUND. YOU MIGHT LEARN SOMETHING!
WELL, I'LL BE! SHE'S BEAUTIFUL.
I WONDER IF SCIENCE CAN EXPLAIN WHY PICKLES TASTE EVEN BETTER IN SPACE?

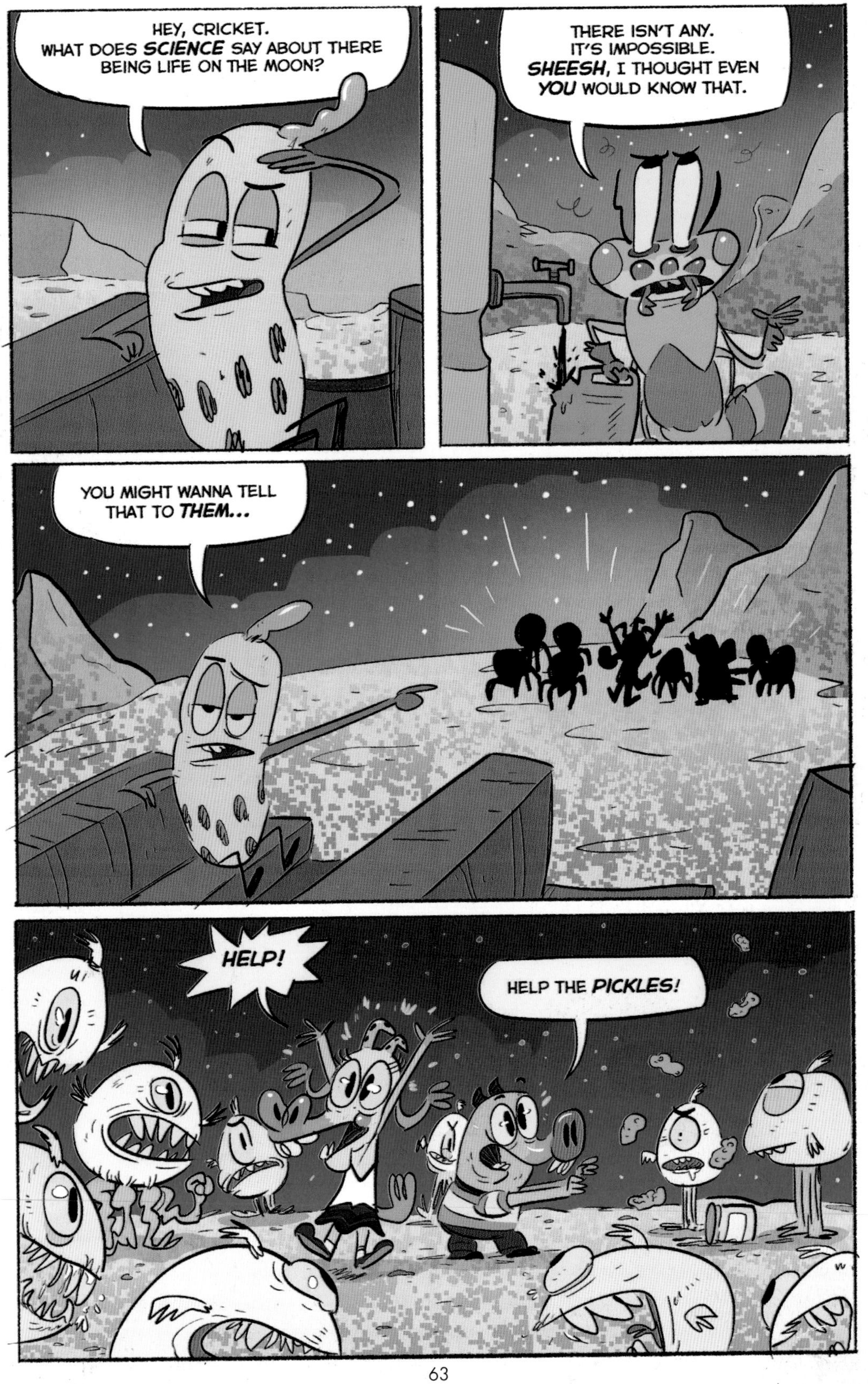
HEY, CRICKET.
WHAT DOES SCIENCE SAY ABOUT THERE BEING LIFE ON THE MOON?
THERE ISN'T ANY. IT'S IMPOSSIBLE. SHEESH, I THOUGHT EVEN YOU WOULD KNOW THAT.
YOU MIGHT WANNA TELL THAT TO THEM...
HELP!
HELP THE PICKLES!

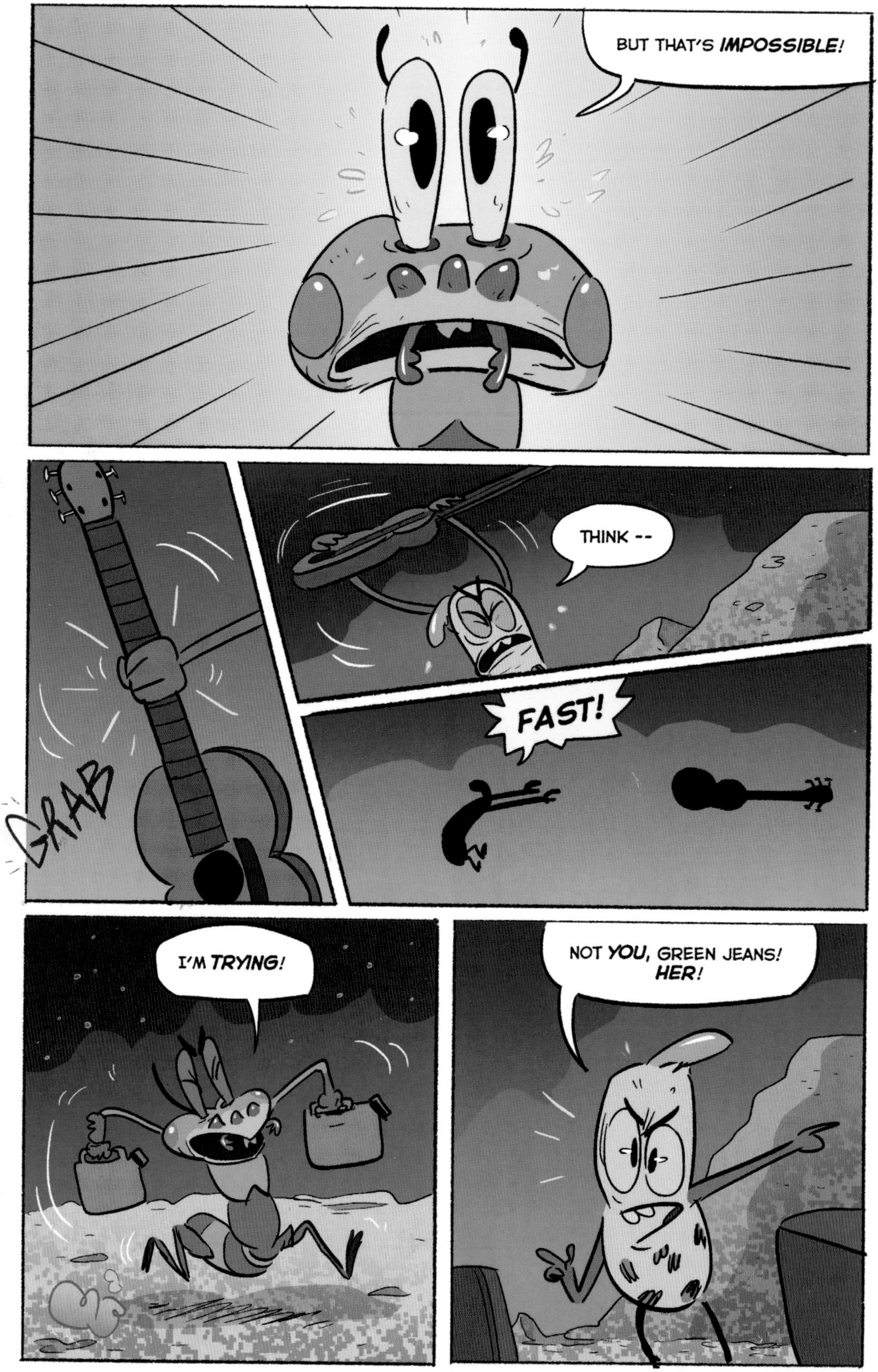
BUT THAT'S IMPOSSIBLE!
GRAB
THINK --
FAST!
I'M TRYING!
NOT YOU, GREEN JEANS! HER!

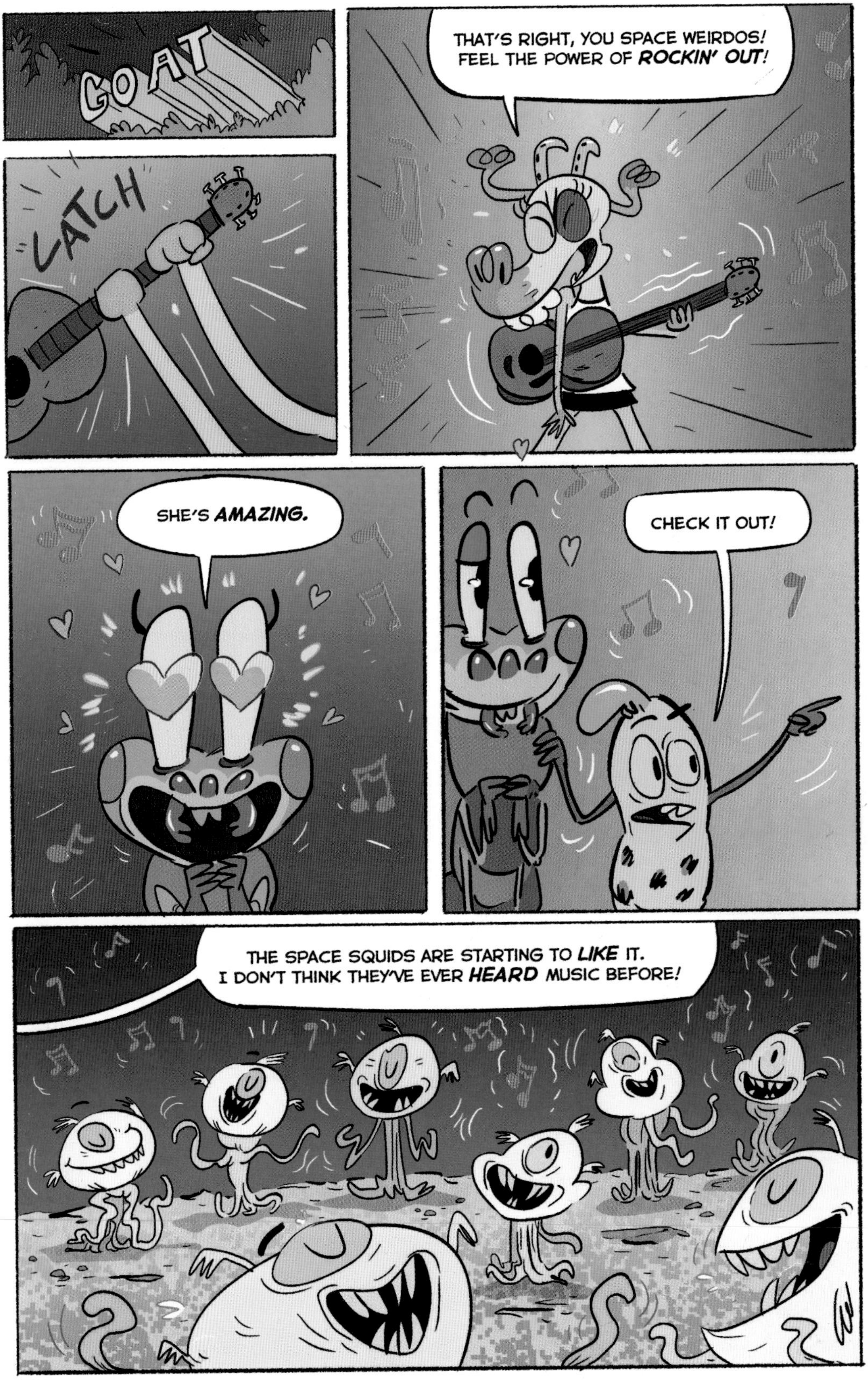
GOAT
LATCH
THAT'S RIGHT, YOU SPACE WEIRDOS! FEEL THE POWER OF ROCKIN' OUT!
SHE'S AMAZING.
CHECK IT OUT!
THE SPACE SQUIDS ARE STARTING TO LIKE IT. I DON'T THINK THEY'VE EVER HEARD MUSIC BEFORE!

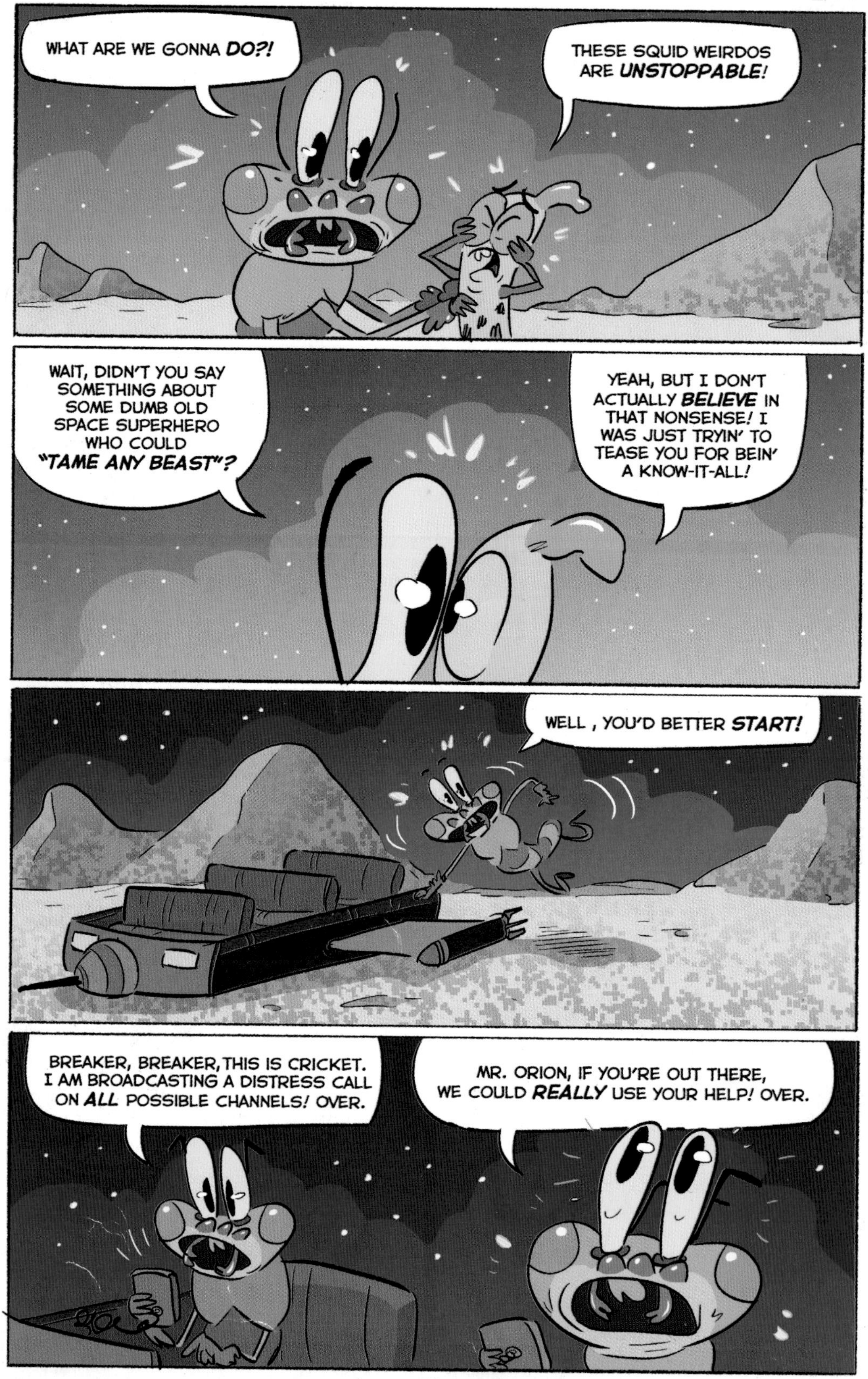
WHAT ARE WE GONNA DO?!
THESE SQUID WEIRDOS ARE UNSTOPPABLE!
WAIT, DIDN'T YOU SAY SOMETHING ABOUT SOME DUMB OLD SPACE SUPERHERO WHO COULD "TAME ANY BEAST"?
YEAH, BUT I DON'T ACTUALLY BELIEVE IN THAT NONSENSE! I WAS JUST TRYIN' TO TEASE YOU FOR BEIN' A KNOW-IT-ALL!
WELL, YOU'D BETTER START!
BREAKER, BREAKER, THIS IS CRICKET. I AM BROADCASTING A DISTRESS CALL ON ALL POSSIBLE CHANNELS! OVER.
MR. ORION, IF YOU'RE OUT THERE, WE COULD REALLY USE YOUR HELP! OVER.

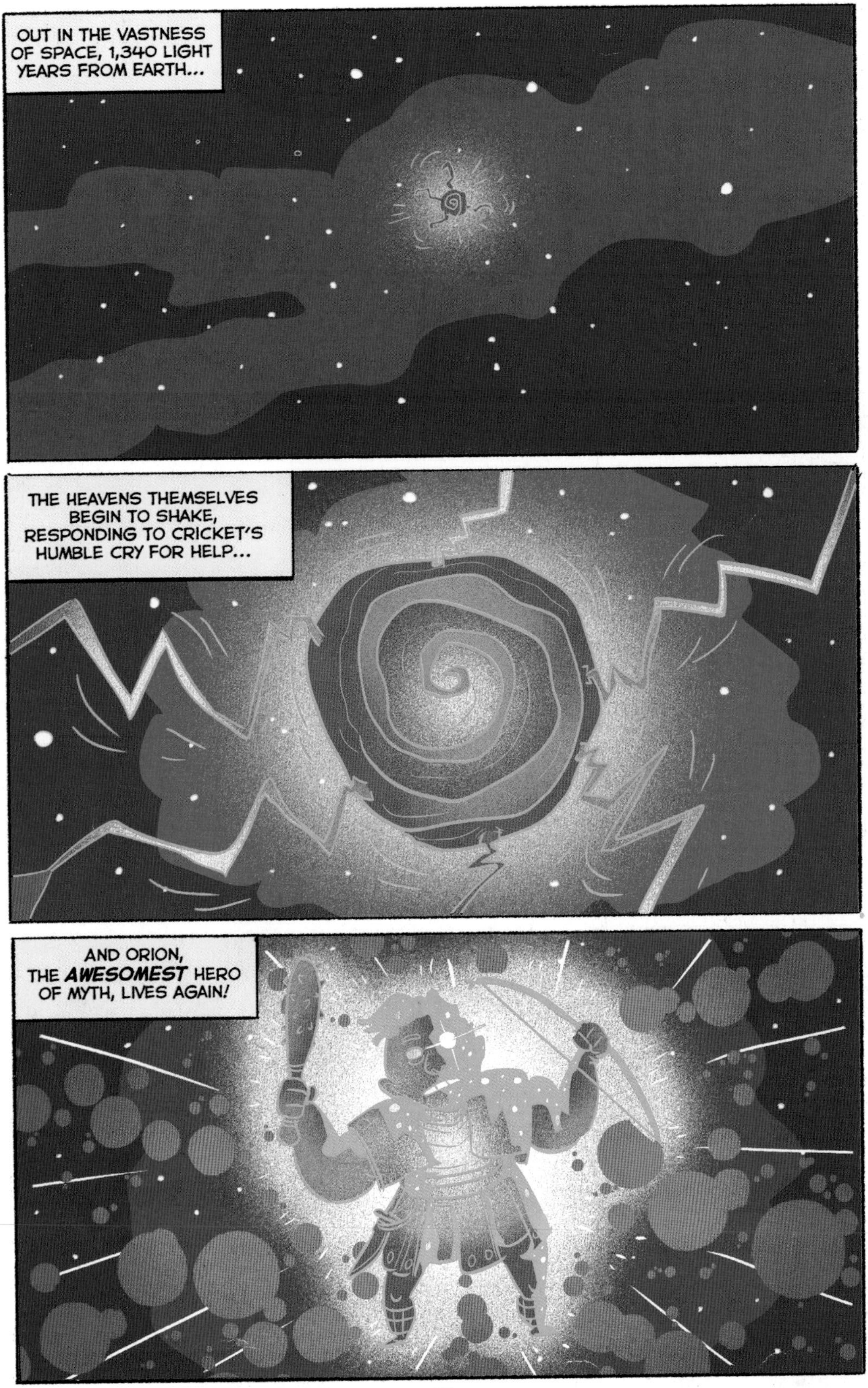
OUT IN THE VASTNESS OF SPACE, 1,340 LIGHT YEARS FROM EARTH...
THE HEAVENS THEMSELVES BEGIN TO SHAKE, RESPONDING TO CRICKET'S HUMBLE CRY FOR HELP...
AND ORION, THE *AWESOMEST* HERO OF MYTH, LIVES AGAIN!

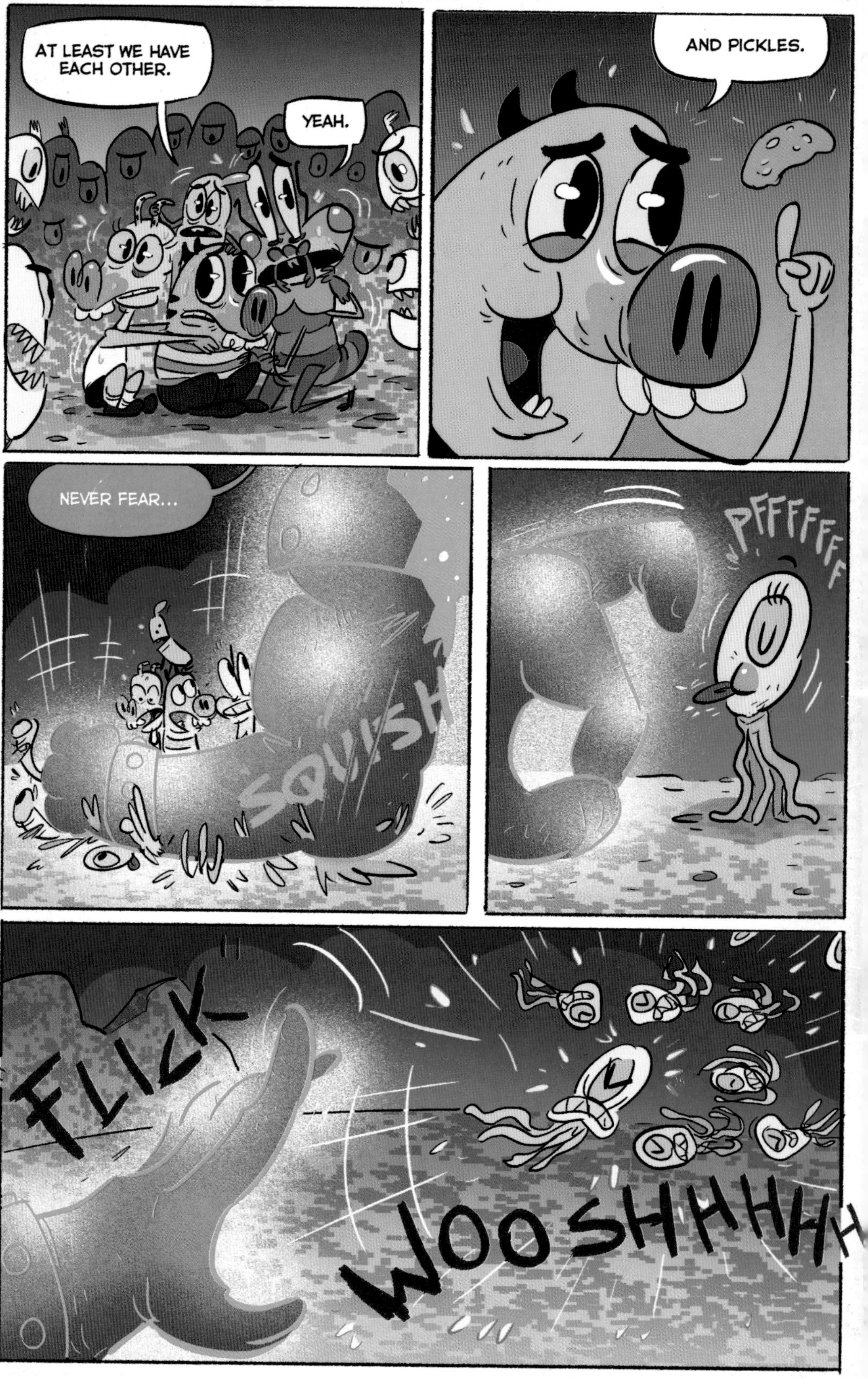
AT LEAST WE HAVE EACH OTHER.
YEAH.
AND PICKLES.
NEVER FEAR...
SQUISH
PFFFFFFF
FLICK
WOOSHHHHH

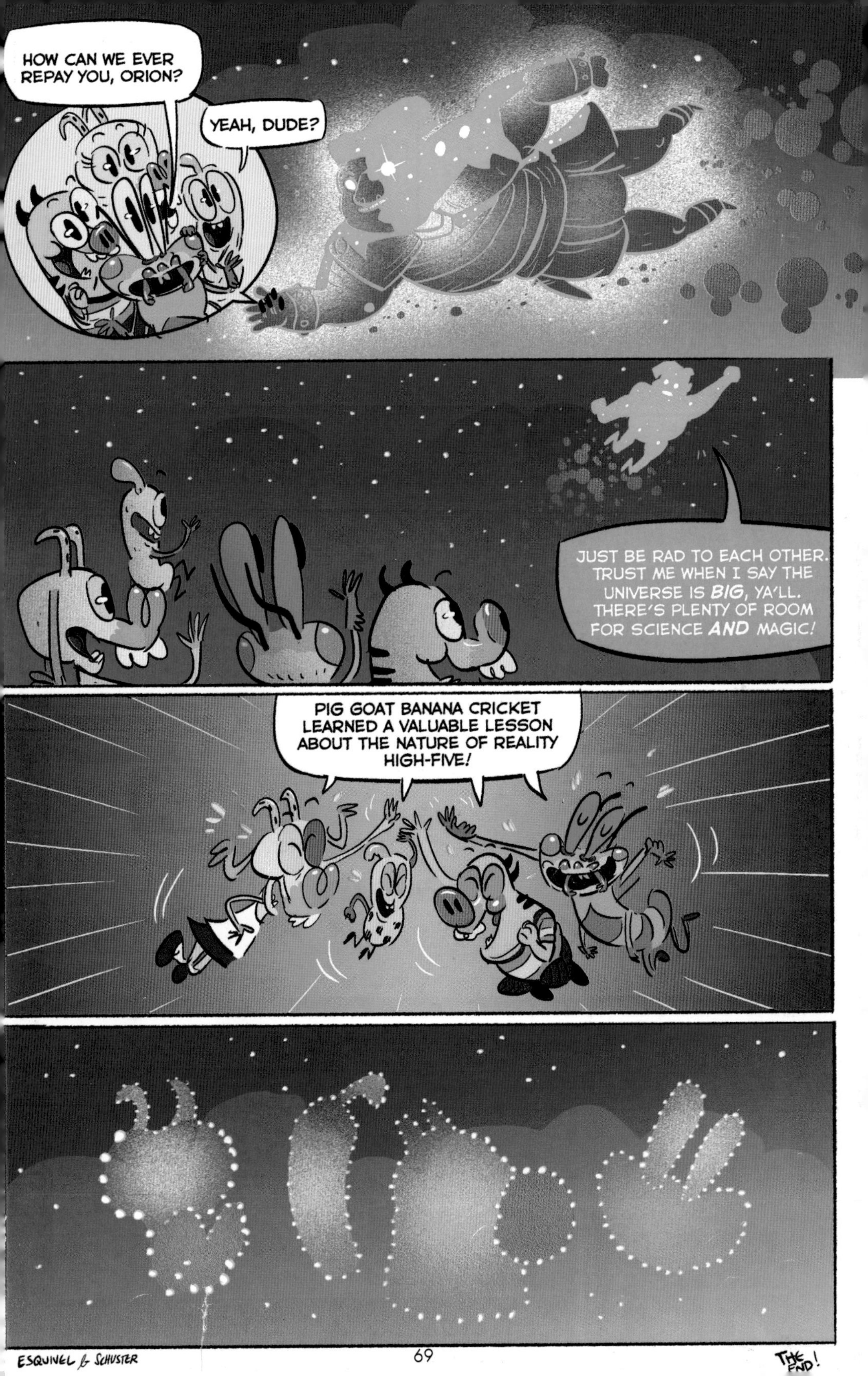
HOW CAN WE EVER REPAY YOU, ORION?
YEAH, DUDE?
JUST BE RAD TO EACH OTHER. TRUST ME WHEN I SAY THE UNIVERSE IS *BIG*, YA'LL. THERE'S PLENTY OF ROOM FOR SCIENCE **AND** MAGIC!
PIG GOAT BANANA CRICKET LEARNED A VALUABLE LESSON ABOUT THE NATURE OF REALITY HIGH-FIVE!
ESQUIVEL & SCHUSTER
THE END!

WATCH OUT FOR PAPERCUTZ

Welcome to the tele-communicative, third NICKELODEON PANDEMONIUM! graphic novel from Papercutz, those smart-phone-users dedicated to publishing great graphic novels for all ages (and area codes). I'm Jim Salicrup, the Editor-in-Chief and not a robot caller, here to offer up a quick overview of the great Nickelodeon graphic novels available now from Papercutz...

For SANJAY AND CRAIG, press one... If you enjoy the SANJAY AND CRAIG show on Nickelodeon and/or the SANJAY AND CRAIG stories in this graphic novel, you'll love the SANJAY AND CRAIG graphic novels—all three of them! Each one is packed with 50 pages of new comics featuring all your favorite SANJAY AND CRAIG characters, including Sanjay's parents, Vijay and Darlene Patel; friends, Hector Flanagan, Megan Sparkles, Belle and Penny Pepper; plus crazy neighbor Mr. Leslie Noodman; and Sanjay's idol, Remington Tufflips.

For BREADWINNERS, press two... Who can possibly get enough of those two quazy bread-delivering ducks, SwaySway and Buhdeuce? Fortunately, beyond the TV series and the stories in this graphic novel, there are two whole Papercutz graphic novels filled with plenty of all-new BREADWINNERS stories! Featuring such Pondgean pals as Jelly, the Bread Maker, Ketta, T-Midi, Rambamboo, plus: Oonski the Great and all sorts of Monsters! SwaySway and Buhdeuce's zeal to deliver bread also translates into their desire to entertain you—they always deliver, and never give up! This series will quack you up!

For HARVEY BEAKS, press three... HARVEY BEAKS is the story of the unlikely friendship between a kid who's never broken the rules and his two friends who've never lived by any. If you've enjoyed the TV series and the stories in this graphic novel, and you're looking for more new HARVEY BEAKS stories, you have to get his two graphic novels! You'll love Harvey's adventures with Fee and Foo, as well as Dade, Technobear, Princess, Jeremy, Randl, and many more!

For PIG GOAT BANANA CRICKET, press four... What do a Pig, a Goat, a Banana, and a Cricket have in common? Nothing! But that doesn't stop these four best friends from having the time of their lives in a weird and wild city where absolutely anything goes! They live together, argue with each other, stand up for each other, and even though their adventures may take them on different paths, they always start and end each day as a team! If you love the TV series and/or the comics in this graphic novel, you'll love the PIG GOAT BANANA CRICKET graphic novel from Papercutz!

For THE LOUD HOUSE, press five... Ever wonder what it's like having a big family? Well, in Nickelodeon's newest animated series, THE LOUD HOUSE, 11-year-old Lincoln Loud gives you an inside look at what it takes to survive in the chaos of a huge household, especially as the only boy with 10 sisters (Lori, Leni, Luna, Luan, Lynn, Lucy, Lana, Lola, Lisa, and Lily)! The trick to surviving is to remain calm, cool, and collected. But most importantly for Lincoln, you've got to have a plan. With all the chaos, and craziness, one thing is always for sure: there is never a dull moment in the Loud house! If you love the TV series and/or the comics in this graphic novel (including the preview on the pages following), you'll love THE LOUD HOUSE, the all-new graphic novel series from Papercutz!

For any other Papercutz inquiries, please go to Papercutz.com for more information.

You may hang up now, or just turn the page.

Thank you, Jim

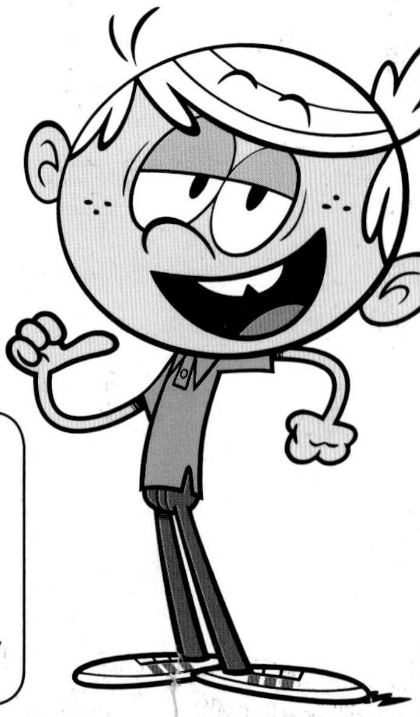

STAY IN TOUCH!

EMAIL:	salicrup@papercutz.com
WEB:	papercutz.com
INSTAGRAM:	@papercutzgn
TWITTER:	@papercutzgn
FACEBOOK:	PAPERCUTZGRAPHICNOVELS
FANMAIL:	Papercutz, 160 Broadway, Suite 700, East Wing, New York, NY 10038

Special Preview of THE LOUD HOUSE #1 “There Will Be Chaos”

“SHOCKER”

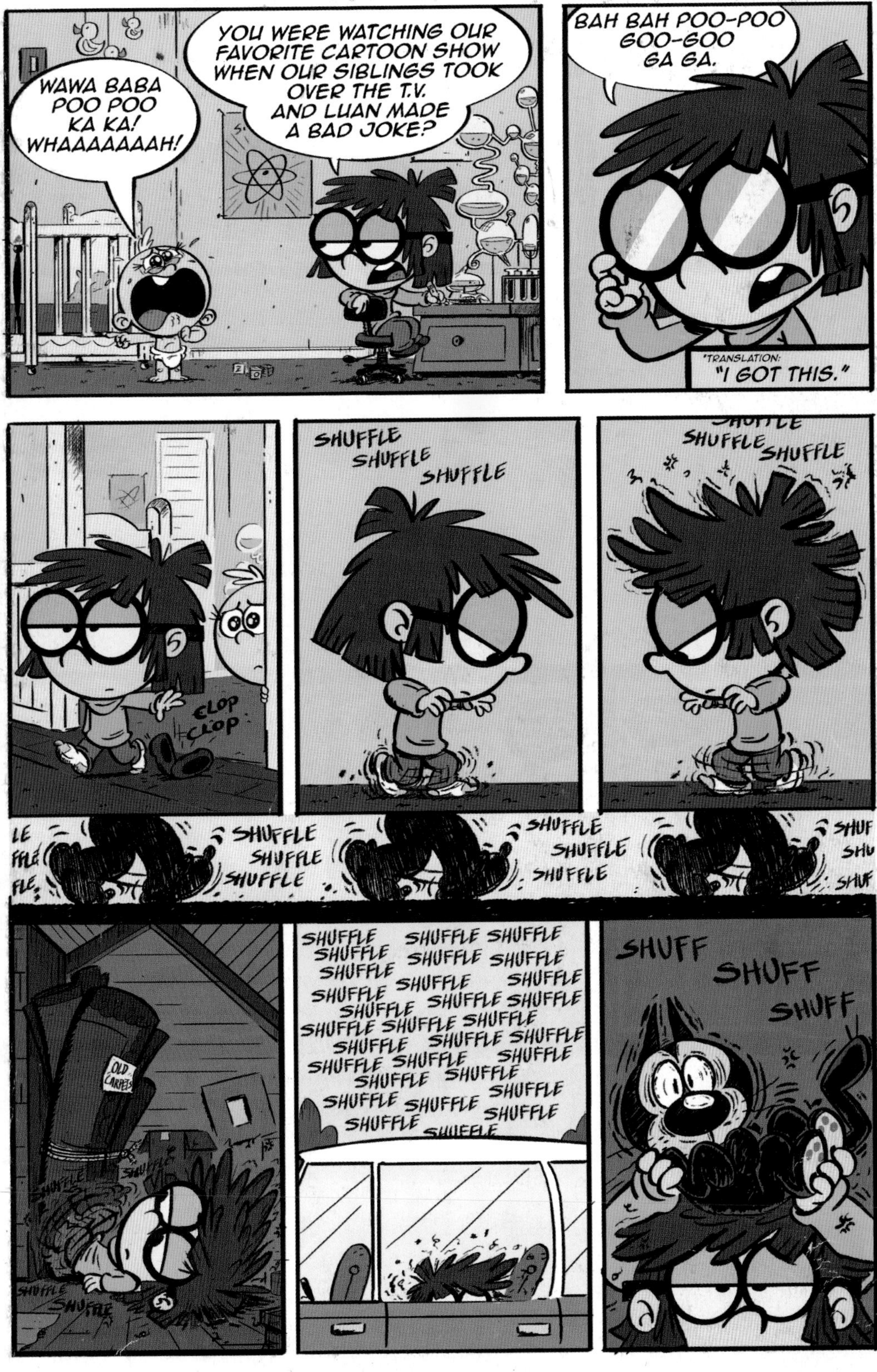
WAWA BABA POO POO KA KA! WHAAAAAAAH!
YOU WERE WATCHING OUR FAVORITE CARTOON SHOW WHEN OUR SIBLINGS TOOK OVER THE T.V. AND LUAN MADE A BAD JOKE?
BAH BAH POO-POO GOO-GOO GA GA.
*TRANSLATION: “I GOT THIS.”
CLOP CLOP
SHUFFLE SHUFFLE SHUFFLE
SHUFFLE SHUFFLE
SHUFFLE SHUFFLE SHUFFLE
SHUFFLE SHUFFLE SHUFFLE
OLD CARPETS
SHUFFLE SHUFFLE
SHUFFLE SHUFFLE
SHUFF SHUFF SHUFF

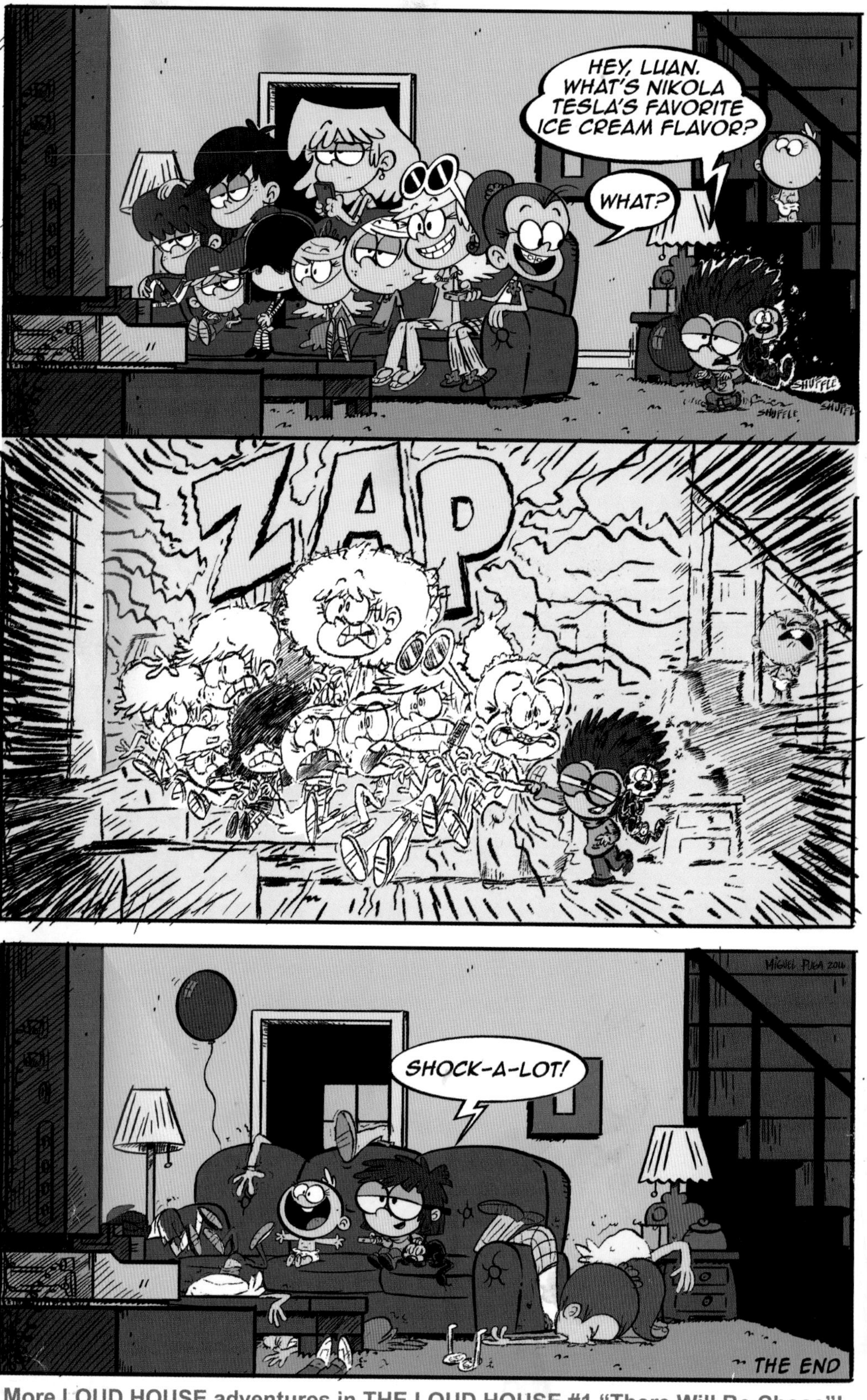
HEY, LUAN. WHAT'S NIKOLA TESLA'S FAVORITE ICE CREAM FLAVOR?
WHAT?
SHUFFLE
SHUFFLE
SHUFFLE
ZAP
MIGUEL PUGA 2016
SHOCK-A-LOT!
THE END

More LOUD HOUSE adventures in THE LOUD HOUSE #1 "There Will Be Chaos"!

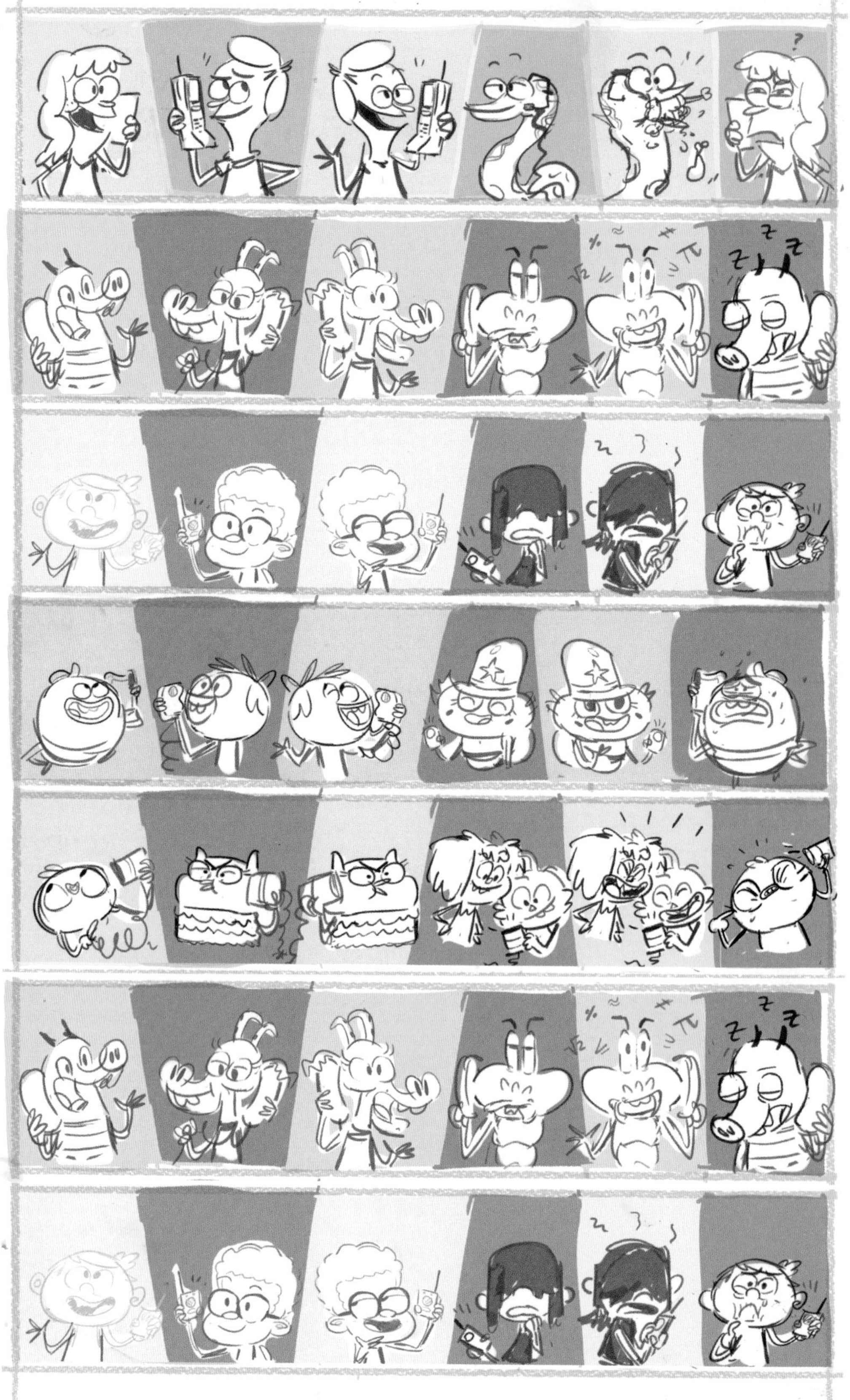